Back at the libr
that the Judge
sitting in his chair beside the ivory-inlaid
table with its pool of light from the lamp
and he was snoring. A thin high-pitched
ugly little rasping sound.

On the table the hookah stood unused,
its mouthpiece lying beside it. And beside
that, startlingly visible even from the
doorway, glaringly present where it had
not been before, was a folded white
square of stiff paper.

He did not need to cross to the table
and take up the folded square at its
corners by the tips of his fingers to realize
that here was another note threatening
with death the old man wheezily snoring
in his chair.

Outside, above the steady chugging of
the ancient generator-motor, he heard the
brisk rattle of Mr Dhebar's little scooter
as it was started up and headed put-
puttingly towards the river. No chance
then to send this square of paper via the
unwitting editor to Bombay for proper
examination by the Fingerprint Bureau.
No chance yet of bringing some proper
police work to this damned isolated, slow,
fish-in-a-tank house.

He teased open the folded square.

Judge. 12 days only remaining.
May the Lord have mercy upon your soul.

INSPECTOR GHOTE DRAWS A LINE

H. R. F. Keating

A Hamlyn *Whodunnit*

Hamlyn Paperbacks

INSPECTOR GHOTE DRAWS A LINE
ISBN 0 600 20249 6

First published in Great Britain 1979
by Collins (The Crime Club)
Hamlyn Paperbacks edition 1981
Copyright © H. R. F. Keating, 1979

Hamlyn Paperbacks are published by
The Hamlyn Publishing Group Ltd,
Astronaut House,
Feltham, Middlesex, England

(Paperback Division: Hamlyn Paperbacks,
Banda House, Cambridge Grove,
Hammersmith, London W6 0LE)

Printed and bound in Great Britain by
Collins, Glasgow

INSPECTOR
GHOTE DRAWS
A LINE

CHAPTER I

HALF AN EGG. Inspector Ghote, flat on his back on the high hard bed, his whole body gently exuding sweat despite the churning of the fan directly above him, found his tired mind repeating and repeating the phrase. Each time it seemed to sound more absurd.

Half an egg.

The Judge, Sir Asif, had used it the evening before down in the tall, book-lined, book-smelling library below. Half an egg. Something about 'If the King . . .' If the King permitted the something of but half an egg. The illicit demand. Yes. If the King permitted the illicit demand of but half an egg . . .

Those must be almost exactly the words the old man had quoted in that precise Englishman's English of his. If the King permits the illicit demand of but half an egg . . . What?

Above, hanging evidently unsafe from the mazy cracked ceiling, the ancient broad-bladed fan heaved its way round once more. Each time it seemed as if, always at exactly the same point, it was going to come at last to a halt. It would slow, all but stop and then, barely moving, bump over whatever small obstacle there was in its works – A grain of heavy red dust? A flake of old yellowed plaster? – and with a little 'bock' continue its weary revolution.

The sound was maddening. Errr-bock. Long pause. Then again: errr-bock.

And its dull-white lazily twisting blades were hardly stirring the thick air. The thermometer must be at the hundred-degree mark. At least. And nothing here in the wide countryside to fend off the relentless sun.

Half an egg. If the King permits the illicit demand of but half an egg, his soldiers will extort a thousand capons. Yes, that was it. A thousand capons, that precise dry voice had articulated. A capon was a cockerel, an out-of-date English word for a cockerel that had been castrated so as to make it fatten better. Somewhere once he had learnt that.

A thousand capons and . . . And then what?

Ah, yes. Yes, got it. '. . . and roast them on the spit.' The old man – that leathery face, those sunken eyes on either side of his curious squashed beak of a nose – had been quoting in English, but the words were those of a Muslim poet. Of course, Muslim. The ranked shelves in that long, high-ceilinged room were crammed with books in Urdu, old and leather-bound. Mostly poetry, the Judge had said. But a good many law books in English too.

'Poetry is the solace of my retirement, Inspector.'

What did 'solace' mean exactly? If only he could be certain he was at least understanding everything the old man said. It would be one obstacle out of the way in trying to offer him the protection he had been sent all this way to provide. But then those elaborate English words were, quite likely, being used with the object in fact of making his own task more difficult. Because if any one thing was plain, it was that the Judge did not want his help.

'I am at a loss really to understand, Inspector – or ought I to call you "Doctor"? You are after all Doctor Ghote, the research assistant, are you not? – I am at a loss to understand why your presence here is necessary.'

'Well, sir, you have, isn't it, received a number of threats to your life.'

'Doctor.' Why had the Deputy Commissioner insisted on him being called 'Doctor'? It was ridiculous. He had no idea of the way a Doctor of Philosophy should behave. The Deputy Commissioner had got carried away. There was no denying that. Giving him some sort of cover story was sensible enough, since the Judge had apparently made it a condition that he should not have anyone known to be a police wallah in his house, and making him out to be a research assistant come to help with the old man's Memoirs was as good a disguise as any. But a Doctor of Philosophy.

No, that really passed the limit.

Then Sir Asif had laughed. A dry cackle in the dry air of the high, faded, book-odorous room.

'Threats to my life, Doctor? And how old am I? Eighty-two years of age. No, it is Allah himself who threatens my life now.'

'Nevertheless, sir, the issuing of a threat to a person's life is a criminal offence.'

And then the eyes on either side of that flattened beak of a nose had momentarily flashed.

'I do not need any Inspector from the Bombay CID to tell me the law. May I remind you that I was a Judge of the Madras High Court for five years before my enforced retirement. And a Sessions Judge before that. And an Assistant Judge before that. And a Sub-Judge before that.'

'Yes, sir. Of course, sir. I did not mean . . .'

Difficult enough to protect a person plainly determined to object to any form of protection. And more difficult still to have to supply that protection while pretending all the time to be simply someone here to help over the Judge's Memoirs, Memoirs that until now had never been so much as mentioned. But doubly and trebly difficult to have to do all that and to battle against that person's apparent resolve to make life as awkward for you as possible.

Errr-bock. Pause, long pause. Then again at last: errr-bock.

And the damned thing really did almost nothing to relieve the heat. Back in Bombay, even if you seldom found yourself anywhere with first-class air-conditioning, at least fans usually revolved at a reasonable speed. But here, out in the furthest mofussil, the generator in the tin shed under the big tamarind tree down at the far end of the gardens near the ruined fort must be almost as old as the dawning of the age of electricity, jerking out its feeble power like the slow pulsing of the blood in the old Judge's veins itself.

It was too swelteringly hot even to think.

Errr-bock.

And what had he succeeded in achieving in the time he had been at the old house? Nothing. Nothing, except getting his one interview with the Judge. And a lot of good that had been. A blank refusal to assist him in any way.

'No, Doctor – it is "Doctor" you are to be called, isn't it? – no, Doctor, I do not think it lies within the confines of my duty to fill your head with a lot of idle suppositions.'

If the old man had asked him once whether he was 'to be called Doctor' he had asked him it a dozen times in the course of that extremely unpleasant half-hour.

And almost every minute of the thirty a sheer waste. Hardly a thing learnt.

'Oh, I realize, Insp – I realize, Doctor, that you had no option but to come here on that absurd pretext of yours. My cousin in Bombay is after all a respected MLA and members of the Legislative Assembly, especially if in their day they have been Ministers, have a way of making life very difficult for senior police officials if their requests are not acceded to. And, yes, my daughter was so foolish as to tell Cousin Iftikhar that these ridiculous notes had been found about the house here purporting to threaten my life. But none of that means that I am bound, as you put it, to assist in your inquiries. Far from it.'

For a few sullen moments, there in the long dim room permeated with the faintly rotten smell of old leather bindings mildewed in monsoon after monsoon, he had thought darkly that surely he did have the right to get answers. After all, there was such a thing as Indian Penal Code Section 179, and he himself was a public servant authorized to question. But all too soon he had, with a sigh, abandoned the notion. Justice Sir Asif Ibrahim would with laughable ease, and at interminable length, argue out the case against and somehow win it hands down. No, the only thing had been to hang on with a muttered 'if you say so, sir' and then to listen once more to the blank refusal. In that bloody precise Englishman's English.

'Sir, could you at least let me examine one or more of

these threatening letters?'

'Certainly not, Doctor. Of their nature they were private communications addressed exclusively to myself.'

'But, sir, it might be possible to tell from the handwriting what is the community of the individual who wrote them.'

'Hardly, I think. The notes were typewritten.'

'Typewritten? But, sir, in such a place as this, remote from civilization, there cannot be – '

'Remote from civilization? Inspector?'

The old man's eyes had slowly surveyed then the fine proportions of the long dim room. They had ranged over the rank upon rank of leather-bound books in the shelves all round it. They had rested as deliberately here and there on a finely carved chair or table, on the pair of tall, beautifully shaped blue vases standing on either side of the wide doorway. They had finally glanced at the fine Bokhara rugs covering the ancient crack criss-crossed marble floor.

Ghote had felt the dark blush coming up from the moment his thoughtless words had been so sharply interrupted. And he had been unable to prevent it at last flushing his whole face.

'I mean, sir, in such a remote locality.'

He had actually had to make the last part of the journey by bullock cart. In this day and age. The plane, the train to the nearest town and a call on the District Superintendent of Police to be assured that no suspicious strangers had been observed in the neighbourhood, then the ride in a battered old hired car, and, in the end, when at the village a mile or so from the house they had come to a halt outside the building of the Rural Co-operative and his driver had announced 'All change, sahib', the bullock cart. In it he had groaned and creaked under the deadening sun as far as the almost dried-up river that marked the boundary of the gardens of the house, had bounced and jolted while the cart's owner had, with much twisting of his animal's thick tail, got them across the river's wide stony bed and at last had reached the big old place itself. Which had been solidly asleep in the beating heat. As it was now.

He had had the devil of a time, too, to rouse anyone. Only at last by dint of calling and shouting in the thick, sun-jellied air had he wakened Raman, the Judge's long-serving Orderly. Poor Raman had received a terrible shelling from Sir Asif afterwards for not having been there up and about waiting to let him in, for all that he could not possibly have been expected to know when this rare guest would reach the house. The old man's anger had raged on so long that he himself had at last felt obliged to intervene.

To be given a look of cold silence which had been his first hint of what relations between himself and the man he had been sent to protect were going to be.

Well, at least in his private interview later he had discovered one new fact. That the threatening notes had been typed. And it was a fact that might well be useful to him. Remote from civilization as they were here – yes, from civilization, from air-conditioning and fans that actually produced some sort of a breeze – it should be possible to track down whatever typewriters were in existence. The notes, after all, if what Sir Asif's cousin, that influential MLA, had told the Deputy Commissioner was correct, had not been delivered at the old house by post but had simply appeared mysteriously in places where it was likely that the Judge would see them. Where, just once, the Judge's daughter had seen one.

Or.

Despite the stifling blanket of the afternoon heat Ghote's mind began to work a little.

Or where perhaps Begum Roshan herself had deliberately placed a note so that she could pretend to find it and thus by bringing in some official police pressure persuade her father to do something – but what? what? – that earlier completely anonymous threats had failed to induce him to do.

But no – the heat must be making him stupid – Begum Roshan could not possibly have any connection with the men her father had sentenced to death in the famous

Madurai Conspiracy Case, and it was clear from the wording
of the note that they had been told about – why had Begum
Roshan not thought to mention that it had been typed? – that
the Madurai case was at the heart of the affair.

*17 days only remaining. Sentence of death will be carried
out in accordance with the law by means of an explosive
detonation. Justice must be seen to be done.*

That, so far as Begum Roshan had been able to remember
and her influential cousin to repeat, had been the precise
wording of the one note that anyone other than Sir Asif
had seen, though he had admitted to his daughter that he
had received others. And its message had seemed clear
enough. Seventeen days from when the note had been
found came exactly to the thirtieth anniversary of the day
on which Justice Sir Asif Ibrahim had pronounced sentence
of death on the group of patriots who had become known
far and wide as the Madurai Conspirators. It had been a
sentence imposed in accordance with the strictest legality.
But, with the end of the British Raj then clearly in sight, it
had been a piece of judicial intransigence that had brought a
tempest of abuse on to Sir Asif's head, still remembered by
people such as the Deputy Commissioner, and had led as
soon as Independence had been achieved to his rapid
retirement.

What had made it clear beyond doubt that the note
Begum Roshan had seen referred to the Madurai Conspirators was the expression 'by means of an explosive detonation'.
Ghote in his hurried reading back in Bombay of the yellow-
dried reports of the ancient case had found that exact
phrase running through them from start to finish. It had
been 'by means of an explosive detonation' that the conspirators had intended to assassinate the Governor of
Madras, and it had been because of that intention that
Justice Sir Asif Ibrahim had sentenced the prisoners to
death. For all that they had been arrested before they

could carry out their plan.

But of those '17 days remaining' now only twelve were left.

By the time Begum Roshan had made up her mind that with her father blankly refusing to have the local police informed, though they had since at a request from Bombay discreetly checked any strangers in the locality, she must seek the help of her influential cousin, the MLA, and by the time the latter had contacted the Deputy Commissioner a good many precious hours had been lost.

Not that, once his own long journey culminating in the slow progress through the baking heat of the lumbering bullock cart had been completed, he had been able to make anything approaching rapid progress.

He stirred angrily on the hard surface of the sheet-covered mattress. He must do something more. He must take more decisive steps than conduct almost furtive conversations with the other inhabitants of the old slowly decaying house, trying all the time to avoid the Judge's coldly caustic eye.

And trying equally to keep up the ridiculous pretence of being 'Doctor Ghote'. Doctor Ghote helping old Sir Asif with his suddenly appearing from nowhere Memoirs. As if anyone anywhere in India would dare, surely even now, to publish the autobiography of the man who had sentenced the Madurai Conspirators.

At least the people he had to investigate in this doubly clumsy manner were few in number. The fact that the threatening notes had been written in English, and good English too, and had been typed had put out of reckoning at one stroke all the servants. Not that there were so many of them now. And he had as well been able to discount such villagers who had occasion to come up to the house, individuals like the milkman appearing just after dawn with his heavy-uddered cow, a bleating calf at her side, its head half-covered in a muslin muzzle to prevent it getting at the milk its noise was helping to make flow, or, from further

away, the postman on his bicycle, white Gandhi cap hardly
fending off the oppressive sun, making his rare calls.

So there had remained really only three possibilities. A
curious collection, and each in a different way unlikely.

First, and unlikeliest of all, though not, he felt, totally to
be dismissed, was Begum Roshan herself. Clearly she had
no connection with the Madurai Conspirators. But, from
what he had been able to gather, in those distant days,
when she would have been in her early twenties at most, she
had not been cooped up in a house in the mofussil as house-
keeper to her father but had been out in the world, aware
of events around her.

Next, there was the Saint. And how could you really
suspect such a figure, a man devoted to walking the length
and breadth of India, with the mission of making all men
brothers? But it was true nevertheless, a well-known fact,
that in those distant days of the freedom struggle he had
been one of the foremost in the fight. Yet that was long ago.
And he had since beyond doubt 'changed his garb', as they
said, put on the saffron garments of the holy man and adopted
the name of Anand Baba, father of bliss. He might be an
unapproachable figure – as yet there had been no opportunity
of speaking to him – but he was not a figure to suspect.
Never.

Yet what was he doing here, in the house of a well-known
Muslim landlord family? It seemed that he stayed here
whenever his wanderings brought him anywhere near the
district. Yet he and the Judge appeared to have nothing in
common. Certainly they were less fiercely opposed than
when one had been a leader in the Quit India movement
and the other an inflexible upholder of the law of the British
Raj. But they were still poles apart. The Hindu ascetic
and the Muslim lover of fine things; the preacher of an all-
embracing love and the fierce believer in a limiting and
restrictive legal code.

It was a puzzle.

But hardly more of a puzzle than the third English-speaker,

possible typewriter-user, in the house. The American. The
priest, if he was a priest, Father Adam.

When he had first met him, on the evening of his own
arrival, he thought he had misheard the Judge's introduction.
As if, with that precise Englishman's English, that was
possible. But 'Father Adam'? And the lean, pale, young
American with his tangle of dark eyebrows meeting above
intense hollow eyes, wearing, not one of the billowing white
robes tied at the waist with white rope that a Christian priest
ought to wear, but a check shirt in bold red and blue and
informal khaki pants with only a plain black necktie loosely
tied as an evident concession to the Judge's views on the
dress appropriate for dinner.

Nor when he had addressed him, cautiously, as 'Father'
had his quick 'Mort, call me Mort' been in any way reassuring. And as for his conversation during the rest of the
evening, it had been more suitable for some Communist
journalist rehearsing scathing editorials for Bombay's
extremist, muck-raking *Blitz* than for any man of religion.

So, although the fellow was plainly much too young to
remember anything at all of the Madurai Conspiracy Case,
it was certainly possible that he felt himself to be somehow a
representative of a once-oppressed people. But why was
such a firebrand a guest in this house?

His one attempt so far, in a wary conversation, to get out
of him at least an answer to that had been swept away,
when he had learnt that 'Doctor Ghote' was from Bombay,
in a wild flood of talk about the iniquity of the conditions
endured by the city's jhopadpatty dwellers in their huddles
of makeshift huts in the shadows of ever-rising tall new
office blocks and apartment towers.

Perhaps some time this evening another try at the fellow
might meet with more success. A cunningly framed, casual
question about using a typewriter. That might hit a tender
spot.

And the time for that, surely, would not be long now. He
must have been lying stewing under his absurdly useless

fan for nearly three hours. Before too long it would be possible to get up and move about with the promise of the relative coolness of evening not far off.

But the case against the priest – if he was a priest? – surely it was scarcely more solid than the flimsy circumstances involving the other two possible typewriter users in the house? The Judge's daughter, with her years of looking after her father, and the goodness-radiating figure of the Saint, Anand Baba? Yet the Judge had received threats against his life. Threats to kill him 'by means of an explosive detonation' in just twelve days from now.

And it was his own duty to stop that happening. Whatever the attitude of the Judge was to him, he had this duty. He had been sent here as a police officer to prevent a most serious crime and to detect one scarcely less serious. Then he would do that duty.

Errr-bock. Pause. And then, when it seemed for the thousandth time that the damned thing was going to stop at last, again: errr-bock.

No, the Deputy Commissioner, old hawk of ancient days, had made the matter crystal clear in giving him his parting instructions.

'Understand vun thing, Ghote. Vat ve have on our backs is not just an MLA only. That fellow is almost as damn influential as the Minister for Police Affairs himself. Ven he is asking, that is ordering. And so here am I, vith heaven knows how much vork to be done, having to find an officer to go and protect that British-loving svine who sentenced those chaps to death.'

'Sir,' he had put in then, those dry-as-fallen-leaves reports of the old case fresh in his mind. 'Sir, I do not think Justice Sir Asif Ibrahim was acting from British-loving motives only. Sir, I believe from what he said then that he saw himself as doing no more than upholding the law.'

'Nonsense, man. He knew that Independence must come soon. He could have imposed some damn long gaol term, vell knowing that they vould get their pardon ven the day

came. Any reasonable man vould have done that. Vy, he
embarrassed some of the British even by vat he had done.
No, no. I do not vish one bit to help a svine like that.'

'No, sir.'

'But somevun I have got to send, and that is going to be
you, Ghote.'

'Yes, sir.'

'But do not be thinking the fellow is going to thank you
in any vay vatsoever. His cousin was making it vun hundred
per cent clear that he does not vish to be helped. But, you,
Ghote, have got to persvade him. I am going to see that the
fellow is damn vell protected, and you, Ghote, are vat I am
going to do that vith. You are the thin end of my vedge,
Ghote. The thin end of my vedge.'

'Yes, sir.'

'So vunce you get there, push, man, push.'

'Yes, sir.'

CHAPTER II

As IT TURNED OUT, Inspector Ghote was up from his high,
wooden-ended bed, all dark swirls of heavy carving, well
before the long afternoon stupor had ended. What jerked
him abruptly into a sitting position on the hard wide
mattress was a sound.

At first he had thought it was only some slight extra noise
coming from the aged fan above him, a new continuous
low groan added to the regular, maddeningly delayed,
inexorable errr-bock, errr-bock that had kept him half
awake all the long deadeningly hot afternoon. But in a
minute or so he had realized that the noise was not coming
from anything in the room at all. It was coming from outside.
Somewhere in the sun-compressed stillness, where every
least bird was stifled into silence, something was making a
sound, a tiny unbroken buzzing.

He sat there on the bed and strained his ears. Was it only the generator down in the tin shed at the far end of the big overgrown gardens, by the ruin of the fort? He had understood from Raman, wide-eyed, scared-looking, shyly-grinning Raman, that the engine ran only when light was needed in the big house and that the stored power of a set of big old batteries was sufficient for such other needs as there were during daylight hours. But perhaps for some special reason the ancient engine had been started up early today. But no. He recalled the machine's throbbing sound well enough from the evening before, deep and reluctant, like the fan grunting round above him still, or like the blood in the Judge's old veins, feeble but formidably obstinate.

And the buzzing was getting minute by minute louder.

Suddenly he knew what it was. He slid from the tall bed, went over to the window and pushed apart the heavy time-bleached wooden shutters. The light of the sun, although it was not striking directly on to this side of the house, struck him like a blow on the nose. He blinked. But, far away across on the other side of the almost dried-up river, he saw what he had been expecting to see. There, under the jabbing glare, moving steadily onwards like an indefatigable beetle, was a little motor-scooter with crouched on it, as if it had a pair of filmy white wings, a man wearing a white kurta on his upper half and below a baggy white dhoti, its ends streaming out in the slight breeze created by the machine's modest speed.

A visitor.

It could be nothing else. There was nowhere else to go other than this house along the dusty unmade-up road, once past the cluster of huts that was the village.

But the river? How would that determinedly advancing rider in the dhoti cope with the broken surface of the river bed?

Standing at the window, eyes screwed tight against the quivering whiteness of the sunlight, Ghote watched to see what this newcomer would do.

Who could he be? Someone arriving by scooter could not have come from very far away. In fact, could have come only from the town. There was nowhere else within range of such a little machine. Some municipal official? Perhaps. Yet the Judge had said nothing, when the conversation at dinner last evening had turned to how few people they saw, about expecting any visitor, and it was surely likely that if someone was being sent to see a person as important as Sir Asif Ibrahim, notice would have been sent to him by letter. And even if the Judge had decided to say nothing of an expected caller, Begum Roshan would hardly have kept silent on the subject. There had been several long awkward gaps in the talk at the dinner table which she had made painful efforts to fill. She was hardly likely to have let such a promising topic go unmentioned.

So who was this white-clad figure on the little buzzing scooter approaching with such steady certainty?

Was it someone with a typewritten note concealed somewhere about his person? A note containing the words 'twelve days only remaining'?

But who could that be? And why should he be coming?

The scooter slowed at last as it reached the top of the gentle slope of the river bank. The rider weaved his way twistingly right down to the broad bed of the shrunken stream itself. Then the noise of the engine – it had become more of an angry whine than a buzz when it had got nearer – abruptly ceased. The rider, who Ghote could see now was wearing a white Congress cap as well as his white kurta and dhoti, dismounted. He seemed to be an individual in late middle age, weighty and deliberate in his movements, though he was still too far away for his features to be at all clear.

He watched him gather the falling pleats of the dhoti in a bunch in his left hand and then awkwardly grasp the handlebar of his machine with them. Then he began to make his way across the river bed, pushing the little machine onwards as implacably as when he had been riding smoothly towards the house. He seemed to know the broken, stony terrain well, changing his course from time to time without pausing to choose the best route and contriving never to have to go through water much deeper than the tops of his ankles.

In five minutes more he would be at the house itself. But who was he?

He decided abruptly that he would go down and keep watch over his arrival. Someone who so evidently knew his way to the house could well be the person responsible for delivering those notes threatening Sir Asif with death. Could well then be someone who in twelve days' time would attempt to murder Sir Asif 'by means of an explosive detonation'.

Hurriedly he scrambled into trousers and shirt and respectable socks and shoes, pushing away as he did so the niggling thought that he had brought with him too few clothes to keep up for another twelve days the standards he had discovered that the Judge expected at his dinner table. Why, he had only one necktie, and that was already looking decidedly creased. Yet perhaps his stay would not now, after all, run to the whole twelve days. Perhaps the new arrival – through his still open window he heard the brisk rattle of the scooter's engine being started up again – would before very much longer in some way betray himself as the writer of those notes. And then . . .

He opened the door of his room with caution, remembering that its seldom-used hinges squealed out a brief protest every time it was swung back at all quickly. Then he set out along the wide corridor that would bring him eventually, unless he once more got the geography of the big house confused, to the ornately carved central staircase. There, with any luck, he might be able to lean over the banisters at the top and hear, or even see, what was going on in the entrance hall below.

Perhaps Raman, shyly grinning his quickly-come, quickly-chased-away, wide horseshoe smile, would come to the heavy house door and greet the visitor by name if he knew him, or ask him his business if he did not.

The corridor stretched ahead, wide, high, its walls damp-mottled, its marble floor echoing clackily to his steps, quiet though he tried to keep them. Rapidly as he could he went past its long row of identical, polished, dark-wood doors. How many bedrooms were there in the whole huge house? Was there perhaps, tucked away quietly in one of them, some other inhabitant whom he had not even been told about? Perhaps there was someone speaking good English and capable of using a typewriter whom no one else in the whole big pea-rattling place so much as knew existed.

He shook his head angrily. Fantasy. Fantasy.

Yet a thorough quiet search of the whole house would be worth carrying out as soon as there was a chance to do it.

He turned the corner, and, yes, there in front of him was the head of the staircase, dark and heavily carved. He advanced at a slithering half run. From below there came no sound, until just as he reached the top of the stairs there suddenly groaned out the noise of the wide double doors of the house being dragged open.

Just in time.

Then he heard Raman's sing-song South Indian voice. 'Good morning, Mr Dhebar, sir.'

He had noticed before that, irrespective of the time of day, the Orderly always greeted everybody with 'Good morning.'

But 'Mr Dhebar'. That name rang a bell. An urgent, strident bell. And, before the newcomer had had time to reply to Raman, the answer had come to him. One of the Madurai Conspirators had been named Dhebar. And it had been a decidedly special one. The sole member of the party who had succeeded in avoiding capture when the police had raided the house where they were hiding the dynamite intended to cause their 'explosive detonation'. The man had, in fact, never been captured. 'The missing conspirator', he had been called throughout the trial, or 'the man Dhebar'.

Could this be him? Could that rather squat, weighty, deliberate figure who had come beetle-buzzing to the house crouched over his little scooter be the very man Sir Asif had sentenced to death thirty years ago though he was not standing in the dock with his fellow conspirators? Thirty years ago, all but twelve days?

A single long stretching stride and he was leaning over the rail of the banisters. He craned down.

Below he saw Raman's curly-haired black head, with at the crown a small round patch of grey where the hair-dye had grown out. And a foot or two in front of Raman there was the inverted boat-shape of a white Congress cap with beneath it the slopes of the white kurta tautly stretched over a solidly pudgy torso.

Yes, a man in full middle age. He clawed at his memory to recall the exact age of the missing conspirator. It must have been mentioned somewhere in those dusty, dragged-out, long-stored reports he had read back in Bombay. But he could not recall it. Not exactly. Yet the missing man had been young, he was sure of that. A man in his twenties. Which would mean a man now in his fifties. And the solid figure down below, standing on the veined marble flags of the hallway, looked very much as if he was just that age.

And he was named Dhebar.

Was the whole business he had been sent up here to tackle going to be after all quite simple?

'My dear Dhebar, how pleasant to see you.'

It was the precise Englishman's English voice of Sir Asif. In friendly greeting. In noticeably friendly greeting.

The old man must have approached without using the polished black, silver-headed cane which he always carried. Its distinctive tap-tap on the marble floors had been totally absent.

And now he had come into sight. A head swathed in the elaborate folds of a white pagri.

But that friendly greeting had in an instant stood the whole situation on its head. The Judge, of all people, must

remember the names of the men in the Madurai Conspiracy Case, must know that the missing conspirator had
been called Dhebar and would be now about fifty years of
age. Yet he was evidently on the friendliest of terms with the
newcomer.

Or was he?

Because Mr Dhebar seemed distinctly surprised, and
even put out, by the warmth of his greeting.

'Yes,' he was saying. 'Yes, Judge. Yes. That is – Very,
very pleased to see you also, Judge. Most altogether.'

What was the relationship between the two of them then?
Who was this Mr Dhebar who had been made so welcome
by the customarily reserved Sir Asif?

He set off to creep, step by step, down the stairs till he
could get to a position where he could see the newcomer's
face properly.

'I trust,' Sir Asif was continuing, 'that you will be able to
stay long enough to take tea with us, my dear fellow. I
know that my daughter would particularly look forward to it.'

'Begum Roshan is most kind, Judge sahib. Begum Roshan
is indeed always and invariably most kind to my poor self.'

Now he was far enough down to be able to get a reasonable
view of the fellow's face, although at a sharp angle.

A jaw, heavy and pear-shaped. Above it a small mouth.
And above that – he stooped so as to improve his line of
vision – a drooping pendulous nose. Just visible to either
side of that were two large brown eyes, looking at this
moment, so far as he could tell, as if they were desperately
searching round for some explanation.

And the Judge's next remark seemed to do nothing to
reassure those eyes, innocent though it sounded.

'My dear Dhebar, you know that we both greatly welcome
these weekly visits of yours. They are a high point in our
somewhat restricted lives. A high point indeed.'

'If I am giving the least pleasure at all to Begum Roshan it
is altogether my honour. Oh, most certainly my honour.

And to yourself, of course, also. To yourself especially, Judge sahib.'

His head was a-whirl with thoughts. Why, if this Mr Dhebar was in the habit of visiting the house once a week and apparently gave such pleasure by his visits, had neither the Judge nor his daughter mentioned him when the conversation at the dinner table had turned to the loneliness and isolation of their life here? Because – he was certain of this suddenly – those visits did not give either of them any pleasure. There had been, looking back, an undertone of irony in the Judge's voice just now, an undertone which he had already begun to be able to recognize. Yet it was plain that Mr Dhebar, whoever he was, and it was clear that he was a person far below Sir Asif Ibrahim in the social scale, did indeed come here on those regular weekly visits. So what could be their purpose? And since, obviously, they gave every opportunity to leave in the house notes threatening the Judge's life, was this the man he had been sent out here to apprehend? But if he was, what was his motive? Why did he want Sir Asif dead? And why was he giving him these warnings? Could he possibly be the missing conspirator after all?

One thing was certain. As soon as there was the least opportunity he must find out from the fellow his full name and as much else about him as he could, and then he must thoroughly check on him.

But already a mountainous difficulty presented itself. How to get in touch with Bombay to carry out that check? A house without a telephone, miles even from the nearest one. He would have to get to the town. But how to do that? Sir Asif, certainly, had a car. That much he had gathered from the talk last night. The vehicle was kept on the far side of the river and seldom used. Would Sir Asif allow him to borrow it? But he could hardly say to him, 'Sir, I want to telephone Bombay to check on a regular visitor to your house, a person to whom you give your hospitality.' And even if he found some pretext to give to Sir Asif for Inspector Ghote to make the trip to the town, he would then have to devise some other reason why Doctor Ghote should need to go there so soon after his arrival. What did Doctors of Philosophy suddenly need that would make a journey of twenty miles or more a matter of urgency? Extra notebooks? More pencils?

'But, my dear Dhebar, you must meet our other visitor, Doctor Ghote, who has come to assist me with my Memoirs. Come and join us, Ghote.'

The old man had spotted him. Had known he was there listening all the time, most likely. It would be typical of him. And, no doubt, that warm welcome had been given to Mr Dhebar with the sole object of putting yet more confusion into his own mind.

He burned with rage. And fought to conceal it.

But the Judge's last remark had, it seemed, caused Mr Dhebar much greater dismay even than the mysteriously warm welcome he had received.

Coming hurrying down the stairs, taking their wide flights much too quickly but unable to help himself, he saw that the newcomer had been plunged into a palpable state of agitation, rendered indeed temporarily speechless.

But only temporarily.

'Judge. Sir Asif. Judge sahib, what – what are these Memoirs? You are not writing your Memoirs. Nothing at all has been said. You are not.'

He was hardly asking the Judge a question, even a blatantly impolite one. He was making an assertion. Declaring passionately that something was not happening.

Sir Asif smiled at him, a quick curling smile under his oddly squashed-down nose.

'But of course I am writing my Memoirs, my dear fellow. I have been engaged upon the task for years. Are you sure that I have never chanced to mention them to you?'

'Never,' said Mr Dhebar. 'Never, never, never.'

His eyes gleamed in a fury of denial.

'Ah, well, if you say so, my dear chap. But it nevertheless remains that I have been steadily at work for, oh, a number of years. And what I have written will, I venture to think, be not without interest, even in these times when standards have been allowed so deplorably to degenerate.'

And the old man turned and began to walk slowly away, silver-headed cane tapping out on the hard marble of the floor with a steady insolent beat.

'If you will excuse me,' he murmured. 'A little tiredness. The penalty of age. A short rest before teatime. You will find my daughter in the drawing-room. I am sure you both know the way.'

He disappeared into one of the four tall corridors leading off the hall.

Ghote and Mr Dhebar were left staring at each other like two castaways unexpectedly coming face to face at the crest of some empty pinpoint ocean island.

CHAPTER III

FOR A FEW MOMENTS Ghote stood facing the heavy short-statured figure of Mr Dhebar, his mind still sliding this way and that on the wide slippery expanse of doubt on which old Sir Asif had succeeded, in so few words, in setting him down.

Then he pulled himself together.

'Mr Dhebar,' he said briskly, 'shall we go?'

Without waiting for an answer, since the newcomer appeared every bit as much disoriented as he felt himself to be, he turned and set off.

'Sir, excuse me.'

Mr Dhebar was standing stolidly just where he had been.

'Yes?'

'My dear sir, I am much afraid that for the drawing-room you are taking altogether the wrong direction.'

With abrupt deflation, he realized that, sure enough, the passage he had so confidently headed for – a large bluish patch of dried mildew on its wall reminded him of the frontier-bound outline of Bangladesh on a map, a vague two-legged, two-armed shape surmounted by a sort of waving cock's comb – was one which he had not gone down at all before during his time in the big old house.

'Oh, yes, yes,' he stammered out. 'I am sorry. I arrived here only yesterday, you know.'

'To assist with the Memoirs?'

Mr Dhebar had rapidly pulled himself together. Gone completely was the evident confusion Sir Asif had implanted in him: in its place was as marked a determination. It made Ghote suddenly see him as a steam-locomotive, long-serving and time-marked, fuelled perhaps by low-grade coal and capable of no great speed, but by no means easy to bring to a halt or to shunt off along a convenient side-track.

He coughed. 'Yes,' he said, allowing himself a little ambiguity, 'I am here to assist Sir Asif in any way which he may require.'

'With the Memoirs?' Mr Dhebar asked bluntly.

'Er – yes. With the Memoirs.'

'I was not at all aware until just a few moments ago that Sir Asif was writing any such Memoirs.'

'Yes. Yes. Yes, I understand that. Er – I believe it was a subject he did not much care to discuss.'

'But now he is discussing,' Mr Dhebar said implacably.

'Yes. Yes, now he is discussing.'

Again he coughed, a long rattly sound. And then at last inspiration came.

'The fact is,' he said, 'that Sir Asif has now at last reached the point where he can see the end of his task. Now he knows that he has enough material to achieve publication – yes, publication – and he feels in consequence that he can acknowledge the existence of the said Memoirs. And that – that 's why he has requested my assistance. Such as it is.'

'Publication is certain then?' Mr Dhebar asked.

The question had been delivered in a way that did not admit of it receiving no answer. In a quick spurt of resolution he decided that attack was the only way to defend himself.

'May I ask,' he said sharply, 'what it is that you yourself do? Why is it that you are here in this house?'

And it seemed that after all he had brought the ponderous locomotive to a stop. Mr Dhebar stood and blinked.

Then, after a second, he plunged his hand inside his stretched white kurta – close to he could see that it was no longer in fact white but had gathered from the miles of red road-dust a distinct pinkish tone – and brought out a very large visiting card, somewhat grimy at its fluted edges. He presented it with a weighty flourish.

> P. N. Dhebar, Editor-in-Chief,
> The Sputnik, A Journal of Opinion
> (Weekly Publication Assured)

'Though on occasion,' The Sputnik editor added, 'publication is fortnightly. Owing to the pressure of financial circumstances.'

But Ghote was thinking: an editor, a journalist, a fellow with typewriters of all sorts all around him, never mind what is his motive, it is altogether possible that he has in his pocket, next to those visiting cards, another threatening note ready for delivery.

'And Sir Asif is a contributor to The Sputnik?' he asked, making a sharp guess.

'Yes, yes. My dear sir, you have come at once to the bottom of the matter. Some little time ago I realized that our district has the honour of having a person of such distinction residing within it. I entered into negotiation. Sir Asif contributes one pungent column per week, or in certain eventualities per fortnight.'

Ghote processed this new information. For one thing, it explained Mr Dhebar's dismay at hearing about the fictitious

Memoirs: he must hope one day to secure for himself any reminiscences the Judge might have. For another thing, the fellow's very approach to the Judge must mean that he could not be the famous Missing Conspirator. But there might yet be some other reason why he should want to threaten the old man's life, and even, in twelve days' time, to take it. Because if, as seemed probable, he visited here once a week, then he would at least have had ample opportunities to leave those threatening letters.

He pushed out something of a trick question.

'I am surprised that, if Sir Asif is willing to write, many other journals all over India do not seek his services?'

The editor of *The Sputnik* did not immediately reply. Various emotions could be seen coming and going in his sombre eyes. At last one of them triumphed.

'I do not think many other papers would be altogether happy to print Sir Asif's opinions. The memory of the Madurai Conspiracy Case is not dead.'

The truth, perhaps. Bitter though it might be to admit it.

'Yes. Yes, I suppose that must be the case.'

Mr Dhebar looked at him mistrustfully.

'Should we go to join the delightful Begum Roshan?' he said. 'The drawing-room is that way, my dear sir.'

The big darkened sun-protected room, where Begum Roshan and the other guests in the house were waiting until the unchanging hour for afternoon tea, looked, when Ghote entered it at Mr Dhebar's heels, as if it was a painting, so still and so silent were the three people in it. Or an old sepia-coloured photograph.

High-backed, intricately carved armchairs stood in twos and threes in front of heavy wooden screens, all scrolls and convolutions, here and there about the big room, the velvet of their padded seats, which might once have been a deep red or as deep a blue, reduced by the sunlight of years to an indeterminate grey. Only the huge blue Persian carpet that covered most of the middle of the cool marble floor seemed,

indeed, to have retained any colour. That, and on the grand
piano, standing, lid closed, in a far corner, dozens of framed
photographs glinting silver. And the only sound to be heard
at this still dully hot hour of the afternoon was a faint
sizzling from the tall windows where not long before a
servant must have splashed a bucket of rose-scented water
on to the split bamboo sticks of the chick blinds which kept
the whole big room in blessed near-darkness. That sweet
rose-water smell struck the nostrils from the moment of
entry.

Yet the three people there – they did not seem to turn
their heads at the sound of the opening door – were not
quite statue still. Begum Roshan, tall, thin, wearing a sari of
fine old silk, was in a state of continuous minute movement.
The fine-boned hands resting on her lap flicked in tiny
uncontrolled gestures, and her face, which the first time he
had seen her he had thought of immediately as having been
eaten away internally by some ever-acting acid, so little
flesh there was on it, jerked in almost imperceptible darts to
left and right and right again.

Ghote greeted in turn each of the others with a formal
pressed-hands namaskar. Words, he felt, would be somehow
too jarring.

The American, he saw, had put on once again the stringy
black necktie he had worn the evening before. And, as
before, it was pulled down a good two inches from the
collar of his boldly checked shirt. He was sitting, too, in a
pose of extreme casualness, the calf of one leg resting on the
thigh of the other. Only the black eyebrows above the
hollow eyes in his pale face were locked in a fierce tangle that
indicated some inner tension.

Could this man, so blatantly unconventional, so radical in
all his opinions, really be a priest? Or had Sir Asif's calling
him that been only another devious way of putting confusion into his unwelcome visitor.

But at least in response to that bowed namaskar the

American did speak.

'Hi,' he said softly, breaking the dampened silence of the big room.

The response of the Saint, Anand Baba, was however more disconcerting. He said not a word, made not a sound. Instead, sitting with crossed legs up on the velvet seat of his tall carved chair, body broad and sturdy beneath his loose saffron garments, he released from the flowing mass of his wide white beard a smile, a smile that beamed and radiated and lingered and warmed. Warmed through and through.

It was like nothing else than being struck full in the face by a wave of feeling that was almost physical in its impact.

He stood there and received it.

'Today is one of Babaji's days of silence,' Begum Roshan said, after what seemed minutes of long-passing quiet.

He absorbed the fact. Days of silence. Of course, many holy men underwent periods of refraining from speech, and it was no surprise that someone of Anand Baba's spiritual stature should from time to time erect round himself a wall against the everyday babble of the world. But such a practice could make life distinctly awkward for an investigator pursuing his duties.

He watched Mr Dhebar approach the saffron-clad figure and offer a deep reverence.

'It is indeed an honour to have Anand Baba come to this poor corner of our country.'

The Saint's smile visibly decreased.

'I think,' Begum Roshan said, 'that Babaji would tell us that it is to the poor corners of our country that he comes especially.'

Mr Dhebar gave her a look of fulsome gratitude.

'Begum Roshan is as always perfectly right,' he said. 'Right in everything that she is good enough to take into her consideration.' He sighed. 'Right even,' he added, 'to conceal from my humble self that her father was in process of writing his Memoirs.'

Begum Roshan gave a sharp little laugh.

'My dear Mr Dhebar,' she said. 'I was the last to know about that, I assure you. My father consults me about nothing. Nothing. If you wish to know about those Memoirs you must ask Doctor Ghote whom they have sent from Bombay University.'

Ghote felt in quick succession a fire of rage against the Deputy Commissioner for having gone so ridiculously beyond common sense in inventing his cover story and a chill of anticipation at what answers he might be asked to provide in order to back the story up. The editor of *The Sputnik*, for all that he plainly came so far below the distinguished Sir Asif in the social scale, was nevertheless clearly a person with an understanding of the world of books, writing and scholarship. How would he fare at his hands?

But he was spared any further interrogation. The mention of the Memoirs had stirred Father Adam. The indolent leg lying across its fellow came thumping to the floor.

'Memoirs?' he said. 'Is Sir Asif going to write his Memoirs? And I suppose the book will sell like hot cakes, just because people will think it's going to let out a few measly secrets. But all the time it'll be nothing but a rallying cry for the oppressor class, just when this country was beginning to free itself of that sort of massive manipulation.'

Begum Roshan, with a quick sideways dart of her head as if to see whether the very walls of the room, solidly there for scores of years, had not crumbled to hear such heresy, ventured a murmur of contradiction.

It merely set the priest off as if it had been a hair-trigger releasing some long-kept-down force.

'I know I'm a guest in this house, and please don't think I'm ungrateful. But a man has a duty to the truth.'

And for something like ten minutes more Father Adam did his duty to his truth. It seemed to Ghote, after a little only half listening, that what he repeated of Sir Asif's views was more or less accurate, at least to go by what the old man had said at the dinner table the night before. Yet he could not help feeling that to blow those opinions up into the tremendous crimes that the priest seemed to think they were – the word 'Fascist' came up several times, and the phrases 'capitalist conspiracy' and 'elitist monopoly of the media' – was exceeding the bounds of ordinary debate, let alone of polite conversation.

But he was only half listening. Because with every attacking word this surprising American uttered, he saw the case for him after all being the one writing the threatening notes becoming stronger and stronger. True, when the Madurai Conspiracy Trial had taken place, the fellow was in all probability not even born. And, true again, apparently he had been in India only for a year or two at the most. But he was showing himself minute by minute to be just the sort of person who needed only to have heard at second or third hand of the circumstances of that affair to have fastened on it as a symptom of all that he felt to be wrong in the world.

So were those notes intended to frighten old Sir Asif into some sort of a public recantation, timed for the exact thirtieth anniversary of the trial? It surely could be.

But, if it was, the American had chosen an opponent altogether too tough for him. His own twenty-four hours' acquaintance with Sir Asif had made that clear. If ever a man was hardened in his convictions, it was the old Judge. If ever anyone would cheerfully accept death rather than comprise by a word on what he felt to be right, it was Sir Asif.

Perhaps, indeed, the old man had long ago guessed who the author of the anonymous threats was. And it was for that reason that he was treating them with such contempt.

But motive the hard-to-believe-in priest had and had. Did he too have the means? Did he have a typewriter?

As soon as the tirade slackened a little, he pounced.

'Father Adam, I am most inter – '

'Now, please. Enough of the "Father". You've got to treat me on totally level terms. It's Mort. Mort Adam. And what am I to call you?'

For half an instant he wanted to reply, shredding to pieces in a wild outbreak of truthfulness the whole ridiculous pretence he had been saddled with, 'You should call me Inspector, Inspector Ghote.' Then he and the American would truly be on level terms. But he swallowed hard and came out with the two syllables that had been asked of him.

'Ganesh. My name is Ganesh.'

'Fine, Ganesh. Now we're just two guys together. So what was it you wanted to ask?'

Evidently some challenge was expected. Something to be crushed with a few more references to 'social justice' and 'the class war'.

'Well, Fath – Well, Mort, I was going to ask only if you are in any way a writer yourself. You appear to have such fine opinions that I think you must at times put them on to paper.'

The priest looked down for a moment at his feet. He was wearing, not the socks and shoes which he himself had felt to be correct in this house, but a pair of sandals, and much scuffed sandals too.

'Well, I guess you're right, Ganesh,' he said at last. 'Back in the States I have contributed to a few periodicals.'

A brief wry smile appeared on his pale eyebrow-locked face.

'I guess my writing was the reason I was sent to India,' he added.

So had he brought a typewriter with him? But before that question could be approached, Mr Dhebar lurched with massive misunderstanding into the conversation.

'Ah, then, Father, you are an authority on Indian affairs? I had not realized. Now, would you be prepared to contribute to *The Sputnik*?' He held up a pudgy warning finger. 'But I must tell you, however, that we are unable to pay any grossly inflated American rates. And also that the Editor reserves the right to withhold publication in the event of any opinions expressed, crossing, in his judgement, the fine line between controversy and defamation.'

'Or any opinions that might upset the censor?' Father
Adam said challengingly.

Mr Dhebar drew himself up.

'*The Sputnik* has defied all censorship from its very
beginnings,' he said.

'By carefully avoiding all real offence.'

It was the Judge.

Damn it, Ghote thought at once. He must once again have
walked all the way along the passage to this room keeping
his stick clear of the floor.

Well, he had certainly caught Mr Dhebar on the wrong
foot.

The heavy-set editor was gobbling like a jungle turkey
trying equally to defend *The Sputnik* and to defer to the
Judge.

Sir Asif in the end helped him out of his difficulty.

'But, my dear Dhebar,' he said, 'in the time since you have
done me the honour of printing my few reflections on the
state of present-day society, we have changed all that,
have we not?'

'Oh yes, Judge sahib,' the editor said, perking up instantly. 'Every week we defy them. Oh yes, indeed.'

The Judge smiled. Slightly.

'Or we would defy them did anyone ever read *The
Sputnik*,' he said.

And with those words a wild notion came to Ghote. Up to
now he had treated Sir Asif with the greatest deference. He
had felt that to be his duty, since he was here for the purpose
of protecting the old man. But Sir Asif had made things as
difficult as he could for him from the very beginning. Very
well, see now what opposing the autocrat would do. To hell
with politeness and respect, those twin taboos.

'But, excuse me, Judge,' he interrupted. A sudden dryness
in his throat had made the words come out in a curious
croak, but he was going to get out what he had to say, come
what might. 'Excuse me, but why, if you believe no one is

ever reading Mr Dhebar's publication, why do you still write for it?'

Behind him he heard Begum Roshan give a little gasp of dismay, and was aware too that Father Adam had sat abruptly forward in his high-back carved chair. And from the Saint, out of the corner of his eye, he thought he had detected once again that extraordinary irradiating sun-warm smile.

'A nice point.'

The Judge's expression was unyielding as ever. But Ghote realized that the words he had spoken were an acknowledgement that his challenge had at least put a finger on the truth.

'Yes, a nice point. And under the pressure of your cross-examination, Doctor, I fear I shall have to make two admissions. Firstly that perhaps *The Sputnik* has a slightly wider readership than I was inclined playfully to imply. And secondly that I myself in my old age have fallen prey to the vanity of authorship. I had allowed myself to hope that the plain expression of plain facts, however few the ears that heard them, would do some good in these dark times, that with lies and corruption all around us a few grains of truth would show up like specks of white on the universal blackness.'

'And the Memoirs, Judge?' Mr Dhebar broke in, an inexorably puffing locomotive proceeding along its fixed rails. 'The Memoirs, are they also intended to wake up India?'

'The Memoirs?'

It was evident to Ghote that the old man, and he was after all a very old man, was for the moment quite unable to recall that he was supposed to be writing Memoirs at all.

He found himself, without thinking, coming to the rescue. But at the same time he was not above taking advantage of the situation to press home the small victory he had just gained.

'Ah, yes, Judge,' he said, 'as your assistant on the Memoirs there are one or two questions I need to put to you as soon as possible. The world is waiting for your words, you know. So would it be convenient if we were to meet this evening before dinner?'

It was an unfair thing to do to an old man. But he had arrived here expecting to receive fair dealing himself, and he had failed to get it. So if there was no other way of inducing Sir Asif to give him more information, then this was how he was going to do it. He must at least get a look at some of the other notes the Judge had received, and he ought too to hear from the old man who in the house, if anybody, had reason to wish him ill.

Well, he had made his bid. Would it succeed?

The Judge stood in silence. He was leaning on his black, silver-topped cane heavily now, and his eyes were so deep-sunken as to be almost closed.

'No.'

It was not his answer. It was a cry from Begum Roshan.

'No,' she repeated. 'No, you must not do it. He is an old man, a tired old man. I cannot let you make him work when he needs to rest. I cannot.'

He felt a glint of fury at the interruption. What was she doing? She knew who he was and why he was here. She must have realized what it really was he had been asking of her father. And to intervene like that. What were her motives? Was she not really protecting the old man, but protecting herself? Was she afraid of what he might say about her now that he seemed to be less unyielding? Had she had some reason for sending him those notes herself? Or was it simply after all that she could not bear to see her aged father tormented?

But, whatever the cause of her outburst, it had precisely the opposite effect from what she had intended.

Ghote saw the sunken eyes on either side of the Judge's oddly flattened nose light up again as if they were twin funeral pyres, almost extinguished, to which an unexpected gust of evening breeze had brought suddenly new life.

'When I require your assistance, Roshan, I shall know that my tomb is really ready for me.'

The words were harsh. Ghote found himself wishing violently that h⸍ was anywhere other than in this big, dim, heavily furnished, faded room. Anywhere. Even in the slimiest Bombay slum. But he nevertheless felt himself impelled to turn and look at the victim of the Judge's harshness.

And for a moment he thought he saw in her acid-etched fine-boned face flaring rebellion, proud anger. He thought that now at last Sir Asif had overstepped the mark.

But it was for a moment only.

And then the eyes looked meekly down.

'Yes, Father.'

The Judge turned to Ghote.

'Very well, Doctor,' he said. 'After we have had tea I will with great pleasure give you an hour of my time.'

CHAPTER IV

FOR THE WHOLE of the hour or more during which the six of them had taken tea out on the broad pillared terrace beyond the drawing-room windows, the Judge scarcely uttered a word. Nor did he eat more than a mouthful or two from the plates of cucumber sandwiches, of curry puffs, of little round cakes with a blob of pink icing on each, which Raman assiduously brought round. Once when the Orderly attempted with a hesitant smile and a curious skipping approach to slide on to his master's plate a previously rejected little cake, he did speak. But it was only to snarl, 'Go away, you damned fool, go away.' Otherwise he sat, eyelids drooping, apparently exhausted almost to the point of sleep by the emotions of the episode indoors.

Ghote, too, ate little. Partly this was because he found he

much disliked the cucumber sandwich he had first been offered – it seemed tasteless as a water-soaked chapatti: cucumber was fit only for slaking thirst squirted perhaps with the juice of a lime when there was nothing better to be got – and somehow Raman failed to hand him the plate of tasty curry puffs more than once. But chiefly his disinclination to eat was because with every passing minute he became more and more worried about Sir Asif.

What if the old man were to have a heart attack? From the greyness of his crushed-nose face, in dismaying contrast to the dazzling white folds of the tall pagri on his head, it certainly looked as if at any moment he might become ill. And if he died . . .? How well then would the task which he had been sent here to perform have been carried out?

But, with the first hints of swift-coming night in the unbroken dome of the pallid blue sky above, the solemn ceremonious meal at last came to an end and Sir Asif at once pushed himself totteringly but determinedly to his feet, the fleshless hands clasped over the silver knob of his stick swelling in every vein.

'Come, Doctor Ghote,' he said.

And, slowly but inflexibly, he made his way over to the open windows of the dra..ing-room and inside. Ghote followed, hovering at the old man's elbow, expecting at any moment to have to catch the frail body as it fell. But, with painful lack of speed, they went through the drawing-room, down the long passage to the hall and then onwards up the equally long passage that led to the library.

The tall book-lined room was almost in complete darkness. Only, beside the Judge's customary chair, on an ivory-inlaid table there was a single lamp switched on – from outside the wheezy chug-chug-chug of the newly-started old generator could be distinctly heard – with next to it the elegant shape of a hookah, put there, Ghote guessed, by Raman, who had absented himself from the tea table some time before Sir Asif had moved. If the day before had been anything to go by, the Judge did not normally smoke at this

INSPECTOR GHOTE DRAWS A LINE 39

hour. But perhaps Begum Roshan had suggested it as a means of calming irritated nerves.

Only would it do so?

At the sight of it, indeed, the Judge seemed to give a little petulant groan. But in a moment this was explained.

'That wretched fellow Dhebar, I have forgotten to give him his weekly pabulum. Inspector, may I ask you to do me a kindness? It's there. Over on the table by the window. Would you take it to him? Then we shan't be interrupted.'

Considerably uncertain as to what 'pabulum' was, Ghote headed across the gloom of the long room towards the table the Judge had indicated. On it, by the last gleams of daylight coming through the open window, he saw three sheets of white paper covered in neat and firm handwriting. Ah, the Judge's article for next week's *Sputnik*.

He gathered the sheets up. And as he did so a sudden altogether convenient notion darted into his head. He had wondered how he could get a message to Bombay asking to have P. N. Dhebar's antecedents checked. Well, he would use P. N. Dhebar himself as a messenger. A few rapidly written lines in a letter addressed not to CID headquarters opposite Crawford Market but instead to his wife at home asking her to take them to the Deputy Commissioner: that would do the trick. And Mr Dhebar would think nothing of posting such a letter for him in the town.

He walked back, calmly as he could, through the long dark book-smelling room. But the moment the heavy door was firmly shut behind him he took to his heels and sprinted down the empty echoing passage to the hallway. Thank goodness, he thought, I can find my way quickly now from the stairs to my room.

The whole business took him less than ten minutes. The letter – to Protima – luckily he had had the foresight to buy half-a-dozen airmail forms before he had left home – was a terrible scrawl, but it would achieve his object.

Coming clattering down the stairs again, he saw that just beyond the open wide double doors of the house Begum

Roshan was saying goodbye in the newly-fallen darkness to the editor of *The Sputnik*. Beside them at a little distance the American priest and the Saint stood watching. He hurried through and handed Mr Dhebar first the Judge's weekly article and after it the flimsy blue airmail form. Then he took a hasty farewell.

'I trust,' Mr Dhebar said, with evident falsity, 'that your work on Judge sahib's Memoirs goes exceedingly well.'

Back at the library he saw that the Judge had fallen asleep. He was sitting in his chair beside the ivory-inlaid table with its pool of light from the lamp and he was snoring. A thin high-pitched ugly little rasping sound.

On the table the hookah stood unused, its mouthpiece lying beside it. And beside that, startlingly visible even from the doorway, glaringly present where it had not been before, was a folded white square of stiff paper.

He did not need to cross to the table and take up the folded square at its corners by the tips of his fingers to realize that here was another note threatening with death the old man wheezily snoring in his chair.

Outside, above the steady chugging of the ancient generator-motor, he heard the brisk rattle of Mr Dhebar's little scooter as it was started up and headed put-puttingly towards the river. No chance then to send this square of paper via the unwitting editor to Bombay for proper examination by the Fingerprint Bureau. No chance yet of bringing some proper police work to this damned isolated, slow, fish-in-a-tank house.

He teased open the folded square.

Judge. 12 days only remaining.
May the Lord have mercy upon your soul.

Short enough. But it said all that it needed to. That there were twelve days only now till the thirtieth anniversary of the Madurai Conspiracy Trial, till the anniversary of the day on which old Sir Asif, then still quite young Sir Asif, must have pronounced in public the identical words to the note's last typed sentence.

He thought rapidly.

Yes, any one of the four possible English-speaking type-writer users could have put the note where he had found it. The window over by the big table was half open. Any one of the four of them out in the garden beyond the open house door could have slipped away from the others in the darkness for a few moments. Begum Roshan would be particularly skilled in not waking her father. Mr Dhebar might have come into the room for the quite legitimate purpose of asking the Judge for his article and then have taken advantage of finding him asleep. Father Adam had been standing, when he himself had come out, at the greatest distance from the others. The Saint, wildly unlikely though it seemed, could on his bare feet have crept up least noisily to the sleeping Judge.

As soon as there was a chance he would have to make discreet inquiries about what each of them had seen during the short time he had been up in his room himself. But there would be difficulties over that. Embarrassing difficulties. He was not there in this cursed crumbling place as a public servant authorized to question. He was only Doctor Ghote. Of philosophy.

No, it was still through the Judge that his way to bringing the case to a proper conclusion must lie. Unless . . . Unless here in this stiff sheet of paper he had a way of by-passing that stone-like obstacle. If only he could get the paper quickly to Bombay and the Fingerprint Bureau.

'Well, Inspector, let me see it. It is after all addressed to me, is it not?'

He looked down. The Judge's eyes were wide open and bright with awareness and command.

'Yes, sir, the note is addressed to you. But may I keep it and tell you what it says? It is quite short only.'

'And addressed to me.'

A flesh-shrunk hand was held out.

He put the sheet of stiff white paper into it. He had considered for a moment begging Sir Asif to hold the sheet as delicately as he himself had done, but at once he had realized that the old man would never tolerate the thought of what he would consider his private correspondence being pored over by Bombay technicians. In fact, it was most unlikely now that the note would ever come back into his own hands.

He watched the Judge read those few, all too clear words and tried to quell the anger he felt at the old man's useless obstinacy. An explosion of protest would get him not one inch further forward.

As far as he could make out the old man had experienced no emotion whatsoever in reading this new threat to his life.

A short grunt was the only acknowledgement that the sombre, stiffly worded message had been absorbed. And then the sheet had been folded – he knew it – and put firmly into the inner pocket of the beautifully-cut white silk coat.

But now was the time to tackle him. It could be put off no longer.

He gave a short cough.

'Sir,' he said, 'it is becoming more and more clear that the individual who is writing these notes intends to carry out the threat he has repeatedly made.'

'Of course.'

'Of course, sir? Sir, have you some other evidence of the firmness of this person's intention? Isn't it that you have in fact some good idea who the person actually is?'

'Inspector, I was merely making the reasonable assumption that if someone declares unequivocally that he intends to do something he must be presumed to be going to carry out whatever action it is.'

'Yes, sir.'

But 'No, sir' was what he would have liked to have said. No, Sir Asif, the world is not all peopled with men and women of your always unbending cast of mind. Yet it did hold one supreme example of inflexibility: Sir Asif himself.

Who, from the way he had just taken possession of that one piece of solid evidence, was plainly as determined as ever, despite having granted this interview, not to co-operate in any way.

However, he must go on making the attempt.

'Please, sir, may we now have a thorough discussion of the whole situation? A person is threatening your life. That to begin with is a criminal offence. Your daughter is aware that this threat has been made, and she is most naturally concerned for your safety. I have been sent here with the two duties of, number one, protecting you from any possible assault, and, number two, discovering who it is who has been making these illegal threats. Now, sir, surely I am entitled in this to your maximum co-operation.'

'Inspector, I have never requested police protection.'

'No, sir.'

Ghote paused, took his life, he almost felt, in his hands.

'No, sir, you did not request protection. But all the same, sir, you have in fact consented to have me in your house.'

The Judge's eyes came swivelling round to him with the swiftness of a vulture's.

'Inspector – Doctor – Whatever I am to call you. I agreed to the ridiculous charade of having you here because I knew that my daughter would make my life more of a misery than she habitually is apt to do if I did not. But you are free to leave at any moment that you wish. Free to pack your bags and go.'

Battered though he felt, flogged even, he brought himself once more to state the full truth of the situation.

'And free also to remain, sir?'

Silence.

In the high, hardly lit room the only sound to be heard was the muffled chugging of the generator engine down in the tin shed under the tamarind tree at the far end of the gardens by the ruin of the old fort. A steady relentless chugging, for all that at each chug there was a choke.

'Inspector, understand this. I am perfectly willing to face

the consequences of my own actions. I am aware that the
sentences I passed in the Madurai Trial brought on me a
storm of opprobrium scarcely equalled before or since. I
am aware that a great many people believed, and still believe,
that I ought not to have condemned those men to death.
But, Inspector, it was my duty to do so. They had been
found guilty of a crime that carried sentence of death and
there were no mitigating factors I could properly take
account of.'

In the circle of light from the lamp on the ivory-inlaid
table the old man's face, which had looked as if it too had
been made out of unfeeling ivory, broke into a small smile.

'Inspector, my duty then was harder, you know, than that
of Allah above. He is all-powerful. He can at His will let the
wicked go unpunished. I am only human. I could not then,
as a duly appointed Judge under human law, go one step in
mercy beyond the bounds of that law.'

A cough. A dry little cough.

'I passed on those men the only possible sentence.'

Looking back down at the old man, he endeavoured to
suppress any least show of emotion.

'Let me tell you something, Inspector,' the Judge added,
with a palpable change of direction.

'Yes, sir?'

'It is a matter I have not put before another living soul
for fifty years. It concerns one of the very first cases that
came before me. I was then a Sub-Judge. It was a trial in a
remote area, a case that had its origin in a village which, in
those distant days, hardly came into contact with the outside
world at all. And it was an affair about which there was
scarcely a scintilla of doubt. But you know what things are
like in those deep mofussil areas. Every witness is likely to
be related in some manner to either the victim or to the
suspected perpetrator, and there is a tendency always to
improve upon the evidence. To burnish up the already
bright.'

The old man's narrative had bit by bit slowed. It was as if, even though he had taken the decision to embark on his fifty-year-hidden account, he had found himself increasingly reluctant to let the kernel of it see the light. Even such limited light as in this intimate talk that had so suddenly come to be.

Ghote wondered briefly whether he ought not simply to stay silent for a little and then to murmur some excuse and creep away, leaving the rest of the story untold. It would perhaps be a kindness to an old man who had been betrayed by pressure of circumstances into bringing into the open something he had for years – for longer by a good bit than the whole of his own life – kept within the bounds of his secret thoughts. He would slip away, leaving the lamp on the table still casting its golden cone in the feathery darkness of the big musty-smelling room, and in a few minutes Sir Asif would drop into sleep again and perhaps when he woke he would not know whether or not he had simply dreamt that he had made his confession. If confession it was going to be.

But those deep-sunken eyes were fixed on his own. And they were still glittering with awareness. Asking not for any blurring of things, but only for a little not-to-be-spoken-of-aloud help.

'Yes, indeed, sir,' he said. 'I am very well understanding that type of case. I am country-born myself. Evidence in a matter which is confined within the boundaries of a single village is always liable to receive such additions and what we call embellishments.'

'Exactly, Inspector. Embellishments.' The old man's eyes glinted briefly. 'And so it was in the affair I am telling you of. Though in fact only to quite a limited extent. However, these were the circumstances. The accused – it was a case under Section 302, you understand, a murder trial – was an elderly man, a God-fearing person of the old sort, by religion a Vaishnavite Hindu. He had a little land and was also the recognized singer of holy songs in the village, always in demand for funeral ceremonies and at the various

seasonal festivals. The victim, however, was a very different
type. Whereas the old singer had been content, as were his
fellow villagers, to stay in his own station in life from his
earliest days, this fellow had by no means been so. He was
born the son of a day labourer, but he was scarcely out of
childhood before he had made himself some sort of assistant
to one of the more prosperous farmers in the area. Then,
with savings he had acquired heaven knows how, he bought
a cow or two, at first in partnership and then on his own.
Later he acquired land. And, as evidence was adduced to
show, he became adept also in increasing his holding without
payment, by subtly altering long-acknowledged boundaries,
by moving small heaps of earth by a few inches at a time, by
digging a ditch a little more broadly. You are village-born,
Inspector, you will know what I mean.'

Again he recognized an appeal, a plea to him to nudge the
account forward once more, even though its teller would
like fate to halt the telling.

'Yes, sir,' he said, 'I know the type of person you are
describing very well. An altogether deplorable sort of
individual.'

'Yes, you are right, Inspector. Deplorable. The breaking
of long-established laws, even though they are concerned
only with the most trifling issues, and perhaps just because
the issues are so small, ought to be regarded in the gravest
light when it comes to the attention of the judiciary. But you
will understand that in the case to which I am referring
nothing had up till then come before the courts. If challenged
over some covert increase he had made to his land holding,
the fellow would raucously deny the facts. He in his turn
would challenge his accuser to take the matter to judgement,
and of course his fellow villagers feared legal process. They
were quiet, naturally law-abiding people: he was aggressive
and dominating. He had, for instance, married outside the
village and the wife had gone so far as to introduce fish and
onions into the customary strictly vegetarian diet.'

Again a slackening in the narrative, a counter-current.

'But the fellow's course of conduct led to worse than onions, sir? It came eventually to murder?'

'Yes, Inspector, to a murder of which he was the victim. And it was not in any dispute over land, but over a more unpleasant business. The defendant, the singer, had a daughter, married and living in the family house of her husband, but the husband's parents had died and the man himself was away for a considerable period during the tea-picking season when he worked as hired labour. Now, one morning, very early, as the old father was on his way to his small plot of land, he saw coming out of the house where his daughter was all alone this very land-thief, Balaidas by name. There could be no doubt in his mind what had been hap-pening, and in simple fury he attacked the man Balaidas with a mattock and left him for dead. As I say, it was almost an open-and-shut case. Except that an aged female cousin of the defendant, the Vaishnavite singer, persisted with evidence that he had not left his house, where she herself lived, until after the time that the body of the deceased was discovered.'

He thought then that he could guess what was coming.

'Yes, sir?'

'Well, this was, of course, one of those crimes in which one feels a good deal of sympathy for the offender, sympathy which one ought never to allow to influence one. However, I was then a comparatively young man and I decided to take advantage of the fact that some of the evidence led by the prosecution had undoubtedly been – what was the word you used? – embellished. So, taking into account the principle of *falsus in uno, falsus in omnibus*, that is "false in one particular, false in all", I preferred the evidence of the nearly blind and extremely aged relative and discharged the singer of holy songs. Inspector, the man, having possessed himself again of the mattock which had been produced in evidence, returned directly to his village where with that instrument he at once did to death his offending daughter.'

The old Judge gave a little cough, hardly more than the softest clearing of his throat.

'Inspector, that woman's life has been on my conscience from that day to this.'

CHAPTER V

IN THE HIGH, almost totally dark library, sharp with its odour of monsoon-mildewed leather bindings, a long silence fell at the end of the Judge's story. Ghote was at a loss to know what comment to make. He could see what it was that the old man had meant to tell him. He could appreciate that anyone, having had at the outset of his career such a lesson as that, might well for the rest of his life be adamant in keeping to the least letter of the law. Part of him wanted then to say, 'Yes, sir, I see now you are right to draw the line against inquiries which infringe your legal rights, that you were right even to have sentenced the Madurai Conspirators as you did.' But to do that would be simply to surrender.

It would be abandoning the task he had been sent here to carry out. His duty.

The Judge, his resurrection of these events of fifty years ago draining him more perhaps than even he had expected himself, sat with chin dropped to breastbone, almost as if he had fallen asleep once more.

At last Ghote brought himself to break the lengthening silence, well aware that the old man was not sleeping.

'Sir, I have been sent here under orders. You yourself, sir, have not the authority to countermand them. But, sir, without your co-operation I cannot carry out the duty that has been assigned to me.'

At the edge of the cone of yellow light from the lamp the old man's head moved in negative.

Yet perhaps in the gesture there was a hint, the smallest hint, of doubt.

'Inspector, I have nothing to say to you.'

'But, sir, yes. Sir, those notes you received have been invariably typewritten, isn't it?'

'Oh yes, Inspector, they have been. They have.'

'Very well then, sir, that can mean one thing only. That the person responsible is what I may call a typewriting individual. Sir, and English-speaking also. Well, sir, there are not so many people of that category within this house. And, as you very well know, no person could have placed this latest communication here just in the short time I was out of the room and you, sir, had your eyes closed to refresh yourself, without that person being also an intimate member of the household or a regular visitor to the house.'

He paused. The Judge said nothing.

'Isn't it, sir?'

A long, long sigh. 'It would seem so, Inspector.

'Then, sir, surely you should tell me everything you know about those individuals so that I can add it to what I am able to find out and eventually come to a conclusion, sir?'

'No, Inspector.'

'No, sir?'

'No.'

Another pause. Another stretching out and out of the silence. But this time it was the Judge who broke it.

'Inspector, there is much I know about each of the individuals who fall within the limits you have indicated. Naturally, more about some, less about others. But there is nothing in my knowledge of any of them, whether to their detriment or not, that is more than marginally relevant at most to your inquiries. Even postulating that those inquiries are not *ultra vires* in any case.'

Ghote felt a dart of pleasure. He knew what *ultra vires* meant. Beyond his powers. It had come in a lecture on law at training school.

But what good was that small piece of knowledge in face

of the once more repeated refusal to co-operate?

'Sir,' he pleaded, 'anything concerning those individuals may be of use. Sir, you must know that from the accounts of police work that have come before you.'

'No, Inspector. Impressed as I am with the sincerity of your argument, I cannot admit its validity. Yes, a fact that is relevant but which a limited or ignorant person could not see to be relevant, so much you may legitimately lay claim to. But I tell you, Inspector, there is nothing that I know, nothing, that is properly relevant to your inquiries. You must allow me to use my discretion, you know. I do not have to tell you how often a police officer needs to exercise that quality in order not to clog the mainstream of his existence with mere trivia. *De minimis non curat lex.*'

He felt a swift wave of shame. *Ultra vires*, yes. But those last words of the Judge's were sheer mystery. Nothing else for it but to eat dust and ask.

'Please, sir, what is the meaning of that?'

The Judge grunted, pleased with his little victory.

'Latin, Inspector. Latin. "Concerning the very smallest things the law does not care." '

But it had not been just a little victory. Behind it had stood all the Judge's philosophy. There was the law. It laid down its limits. Within them there was no reason to budge by one inch.

He straightened his back and turned to go.

'Then I will see you later, sir.'

'Yes, later, Inspector. Doctor.'

But before he had reached the heavy teak-wood door flanked by its two tall blue vases, the Judge spoke again.

'There is something you could do for me, my dear chap.'

'Yes, Sir Asif?'

A wind-touched cinder, believed dead, glows again?

'Raman, my dear chap. If you can rout him out, would you send him to me? The damn fellow's been with me more than thirty years and he is still never where he's wanted when he's wanted.'

The old man ended the request on a note of spiralling anger. It hurt. More almost certainly than it was going to hurt shyly darting Raman when he had found him and sent him to attend to the Judge's wants. The fellow must get a dozen such shellings a day.

And at that moment the Orderly appeared, evidently having been waiting within sound of Sir Asif's voice. His sudden-come, sudden-gone horseshoe grin as they passed in the tall, dimly-lit passage seemed to show already a bland unconcern at the rage awaiting him.

Walking still a little sadly away, he heard the unreasoning old voice raised again in as yet unquenched anger. 'You will never learn, will you . . .? Why has this hookah been left here? Did I give orders . . .? And don't you attempt to give notice ever again . . . Why do I have to put up with such appalling lack of intelligence?'

He sighed.

But there was no time to indulge in feelings of mild sorrow. With Raman out of the way and all the other servants at this time of the evening securely in the kitchen or in their quarter, with Begum Roshan and the other two almost certainly sitting together in the drawing-room, now was as good a chance as he was likely to get to carry out that search of the house he had earlier promised himself.

If Sir Asif was not going to co-operate, then he must once more take matters into his own hands. And though perhaps the most useful thing now would be to put a few questions about what exactly had taken place during the time that that last note had been put beside the sleeping Judge, this was something a guest Doctor of Philosophy could hardly do with all the people he wished to interview together in the one room.

No, seize the opportunity and carry out that search.

With each of the four possible typewriter users in a different way unlikely as the person threatening Sir Asif's life, the notion of there being under the wide-spreading flat roof of the big old house someone else, for some reason, hidden, became moment by moment more attractive. Say there was some member of the household whom the Judge did not want him to know about. Nothing easier than to put them in some isolated room upstairs somewhere, perhaps in the apparently disused wing parallel to the one where his own room was, and to have Raman, faithful Raman, take him meals there for the length of his own stay. And, come to think of it, the day before, when the routine of the house had been less clear, he had actually seen the Orderly carrying just such a tray. A large tray covered with a draped white cloth.

And, he realized, there was now a moon to search by. Its light was shining clearly in through the barred windows on either side of the wide double doors of the house. He would be able to go from room to room above without needing to switch on any give-away electric light, if lights there were in some of the remoter parts of the place.

Silently as he could, he went up the wide carved staircase. Best now after all to avoid Begum Roshan or any of the others.

At the top he made straight for the door leading to the part of the house he had understood to be no longer in use. Had it formerly been the forbidden zenana quarter? Perhaps in her young days Begum Roshan had been confined there with the other women of the household, peeping out at the goings-on below, whispering, surmising, giggling? It was likely enough.

Certainly the rooms here now would be empty and deserted, to go by the number of whitey-yellow flakes of ceiling plaster lying on the floor in front of him, looking in the broken moonlight coming in through the stone-traceried upper windows like so many fallen petals from some great waxy white flowering shrub.

He came to the first of the rooms leading off the long passage. He looked at its door. Not a trace of electric light at its edges. He stepped up close and put an ear to one of the panels. A minute passed. Another half minute. Not a sound from inside.

Gently he tried the doorknob. It turned, a little stiffly. Very quietly he eased the tall, heavy door forward. There came the beginnings of a grinding squeak. He froze into stillness.

But the room beyond the slit-open door was clearly empty. He took a quick look this way and that along the high moonshiny corridor. No one. Nothing.

He pushed the door wide – long grating groan – and stepped inside. By the dim light coming in through the shuttered window he was able to make out a bed, just such another as the one he had spent all the afternoon on under the reiterated errr-bock of his fan. Its white-covered mattress was bare. Against a wall he saw a big dark old almirah, its front intricately carved. He moved across to it over the bare stone floor and tried its doors. They swung open with a lurch. Bare blackness inside.

Opposite there was another door, leading to a bathroom if the arrangement of his own room was anything to go by. He crossed over and, still taking careful precautions, slowly opened it. It was harder to see inside the small cubicle beyond, but he waited patiently till his eyes had adjusted to its darkness. There was nothing to see, however. No figure clamped in hiding up against the wall, only a tin bath with a wooden stool in it on which, in some far past day, the bath-taker had sat while a servant had poured water over them. That and a heavy-legged dark teak commode.

Well, it was unlikely that anyone had been concealed – if there was anybody concealed anywhere at all – in the room nearest the door cutting off the old zenana quarter.

So try the next room along.

Again he looked for any tell-tale line of light at the door edge. Again he listened. Again there was no sign of any human presence. With rather less caution he swept the door wide. The room he saw was the exact fellow of its neighbour.

Except – He paused in the dimness. Except that it smelt different.

Yes.

He stepped further in. And then, down on the floor, not far from the window, he saw what had caused the high, faintly unpleasant odour. It was the body of a long-dead squirrel. The broad black stripe down its back was clearly visible in the dim light coming in where one of the shutters was broken.

He took a quick, conscientious glance into the bathroom and moved on. No one was going to inhabit a room with that little sharply smelling corpse for company.

But in each of the other rooms that he went into, taking each time the same precautions, the answer was the same. No one. Nothing. Some, he found, were totally bare. Most still had their bed there, each of them carved differently, and an almirah and little else. All but two had bathrooms. As he progressed along one passage and then down another, the air of neglect grew stronger. Once, where evidently the roof above had some long-unrepaired crack in it, the mattress on the bed, perhaps drenched year after year in the monsoon downpours, had rotted right away in its centre. In the very last room for one moment he had stiffened in alarm when the creak of the door opening had produced a swift movement inside. But it had been only rats, disturbed in the nest they had inhabited for generations of rat-life in a long sausage-shaped bolster that had been left alone on the bare bedframe.

Never anywhere did he see the smallest trace of recent human occupation.

Well then, perhaps this one person extra was hidden in the inhabited part of the house. Right under his own nose. If it was Sir Asif who was doing the hiding – but what nonsense it was to assume that there was anybody hidden – then it would be typical of his attitude to have put the unwelcome cat so near his mouse.

CHAPTER VI

TREADING THE dangerously noisy stone floor of the old zenana quarter more and more carefully, Ghote returned to the starting point of his search and then, with a small squaring of his shoulders, began its second phase, in the more inhabited upstairs rooms of the old house, the mouse-holes near the intruder cat's allocated lair.

The first door he came to – no trace of light from inside – proved to be that of Sir Asif himself. The room was almost as bare as any of the ones on the zenana side. Only a fine Mirzapur rug indicated that unprotected feet ever walked on its smooth floor. And only a small tilted bookstand on the bedside teapoy containing half-a-dozen volumes of Urdu verse showed who it was in particular who lay on the high bed during the long, blanketingly hot afternoons, who slept, or did not sleep, there during the scarcely less hot nights.

Did his fan, too, go errr-bock, errr-bock ceaselessly from after the tired ceremony of luncheon till nearly time for the tired ceremony of tea? It certainly looked every bit as old as the one in his own room and seemed to lean a little away from the ceiling in much the same fashion too, leaving a thin black rim between its white-into-cream casing and the chalky white of the crack-veined ceiling.

And under that fan did the old man dream, he asked himself as cautiously he pulled the tall door closed behind him, his search completed. Did he in dreams see himself setting free again and again the old Vaishnavite singer of holy songs? Authorizing again and again the release of certain material evidence, namely one mattock?

He almost forgot to take any precautions before pushing open the next door along.

What if it had been Begum Roshan's room, and she had been there inside it? What could he have said, barging in on her without even a knock? She would like it only a little less than her father, the thought of having a spy in the house, even though he was a spy she herself had been responsible for summoning here.

But there was no thin line of light at the door's edge, and when he listened no sound at all came from inside. Once more – for the eighteenth time? For the nineteenth? – he eased a doorknob round and then as stealthily pushed a door open quarter-inch by quarter-inch.

In the filtered moonlight he saw at once that he was in a feminine room and one much more furnished than any he had been in up to now. The diffused rays caught the glint of silver-topped jars and brushes on the large dressing-table by the window. The bed had a silk cover in a pattern of silver and blue, its bolster too was covered in the same material.

Yet he knew at once that this was not Begum Roshan's room. For one thing he was certain that her father, never slow to express the irritation she often caused him, would not tolerate her occupying a room next to his own. But there was another, more immediate, reason for his instant knowledge. It was plain that the room had stayed untouched by any hand for a very long time.

It had been a series of tiny things that had given him it – the too stiff folds of the bedcover, the unnatural neatness of the silver brushes and jars on the dressing-table, and even though nothing could be clearly seen in the indirect pale light, a pervasive softness everywhere that spoke of a fine layer of long-accumulating reddish dust from which nothing had escaped.

Then, in a corner that the moonlight did not reach, he made out that in front of what should have been a full-length mirror in the door of the almirah, there was hung a length of white cotton material. And, yes, on the mirror of the dressing-table, directly in front of the window, there was more cotton sheeting. At once he knew what room this had been: the one that Sir Asif had shared long, long ago with his wife.

Except for those veiled mirrors, it had been preserved exactly as it had been when she had been alive.

Or, no. No, it had not. Not quite. In a corner on the far side of the bed, he saw now, there was a pile of small wooden crates. Containers of some sort. And they had been stored here. Pushed in out of the way by some servant, Raman probably, who had been told to dispose of them.

He walked round the bed and bent to take a closer look. The top one, which had had its cover prised off and only loosely replaced, was filled, he saw, with wood shavings, and nestling among them, plainly untouched since it had been delivered from some department store in Bombay many years before, there was an ornate table lamp.

Lady Ibrahim must have sent for it, and then, before it had at last been delivered, her death had come.

And Sir Asif at once had moved out of the room and had given orders that it should be kept exactly as it had been during her lifetime. But he had never ventured back in to see whether his orders had been obeyed. So Raman, or whichever other servant it had been, had taken advantage of that to put these half-dozen awkward unwanted crates there out of his master's sight. If ever Sir Asif did enter this shrine, what a tongue-lashing Raman would get. And accept patiently, no doubt, as it seemed that he accepted every other occasion when Sir Asif's bitterness broke over his defenceless head. Thirty years and more of such trouncings.

He sighed.

But nevertheless he took good care to go into the adjoining bathroom – the bath had a rim of red rust all round its bottom inch – and to open the shrouded mirror-door of the double-size almirah. It was after all a piece of furniture easily big enough for someone to hide in.

But it did not contain some mysterious person – Who would Sir Asif wish to conceal from him? And why? – only rank upon rank of saris, in silk, in brocade, in finest cottons, and among them what must have been Lady Ibrahim's wedding sari, a shimmering white pearl-patterned garment with an intricate silver border deep at its edge.

But it had not been 'Lady Ibrahim' then. It had been 'Mrs Ibrahim', wife of a rising young pleader with all the world before him.

Quietly he closed the almirah's door and left.

The next occupied room he came to, he found when he had cautiously entered, was that which had been given to young Father Adam – no, in the privacy of his own mind he would not call him Mort – and for a moment he was tempted to make a thorough search among the heaps of papers and dozens of books littered about, almost all of which he would have classified as 'subversive literature' had he encountered them while carrying out an investigation back in Bombay, to see if he could find some link between the young American and the time-smothered Madurai Conspiracy. Or perhaps there would be some document that showed the fellow was not after all a priest.

But the possibility of the suspect himself suddenly coming up to his room and finding the Doctor of Philosophy burrowing among his private papers was not to be contemplated.

Two more bare unoccupied rooms came next, bare beds, empty almirahs echoing when he put his head into them, bathrooms bone-dry.

Then came the room evidently given to the Saint, although there was little sign of use in it other than the fact that the bedcover had been taken off and folded to make a bed on the hard stone of the floor. But what exactly was such a person as this doing here? Though warranted as beyond all suspicion, he was certainly oddly out of place in this remote yet worldly household.

He shook his head.

Next came his own room and three more unoccupied ones, none of which showed any sign of habitation. In one, rats or some other creatures had chewed off all the insulation from the wires running down to the switch-block and the bare copper glinted rose-pink in the moonlight. Then he came at last to the one remaining door.

And here there was a thin outline of bright light, unmistakable even from a distance of a few yards in the largely dark passage.

Was this his man at last?

But, no. He had not yet seen Begum Roshan's room. So this must be that. And she herself must be there behind this door and not downstairs with the others. Was she, even at this moment in this isolated end of the big house, setting up a typewriter, usually kept concealed in the bottom of her almirah?

He stood, still as the thick round-headed newel post at the foot of the broad staircase down below, and listened hard, his ear not six inches from the door and its rim of light. Would he begin to hear soon the surreptitious click-click-clicking of an inexpertly used machine?

But there was nothing. Nothing but faint in the distance the choked throbbing of the old generator engine.

Well, there was something else he could do, since Begum Roshan was up here alone. He could ask her what exactly had taken place out beside the doors to the house in those few minutes when Sir Asif had been left alone and sleeping in the library and the latest note – twelve days only remaining – had been put there beside him.

He summoned up a little courage and gave a brisk knock on the solid teak in front of him.

There was a silence, a longish silence – Was a typewriter being hurriedly hidden away? – and then Begum Roshan's voice came calling with a faint note of unease: 'Who is it?'

He went in without answering. Would he catch her just straightening up from some drawer, just closing the almirah?

But he found her sitting in apparent tranquillity on a stool in front of her dressing-table. And there was no sign, as far as a rapid glance could tell him, of anything out of place in the room.

'Excuse me, madam,' he said quickly. 'I very much needed

to see you at a time when no one else was near, and I therefore came up here. I hope I am not incommoding?'

'No, Inspector. No. You are right. We should have a talk.'

'Yes, madam. Perhaps even more urgently than you think. There has been a new development.'

'Another note?'

The eyes in her acid-eaten face darted quickly from side to side.

Should she have guessed what 'the development' he had deliberately not specified was? Well, it was not unreasonable. He had not had time to frame his words more carefully.

'Yes, madam, another note. And it seems to me most likely that it was left by one of the guests here in the house.'

'One of the – But, no. No, Inspector. That is impossible.'

'Impossible? But why, madam?'

'Inspector, they are my father's guests.'

He wanted to laugh, though not with amusement. To find the daughter such an echo of the father.

He stiffened himself a little.

'Madam, believe me, I have good reason for my suspicions. Would you be so good as to tell me exactly where each of those guests was in the ten minutes or so before I myself came out and joined you just as Mr Dhebar was about to depart?'

She did not immediately answer.

Is she going to play her father to the end towards me, he wondered. Is she already regretting a perhaps impulsive move in summoning police assistance through her influential Bombay cousin?

Or is she thinking hard how to cover up her own quick journey along to the library where for whatever devious purposes she herself left her father that threatening note?

But her silence did not last long.

'Inspector, I realize how important what I can tell you may be. But – But you will think me a great fool, but I cannot really help you. I – I was upset when Mr Dhebar announced at last that he was going to leave. My father –

What went on during tea – Oh, won't you understand?'

The fleshless face looked yet more worn.

'Madam, I think I do understand.'

'Yes? Yes, Inspector? Then you will see that I was not in a fit state, not in a fit state at all, to notice who was there and who was not, whether someone, Anand Baba even, slipped away while I was thinking about – about other things.'

Ghote sighed.

So he was not going to get anywhere. But make sure that she really did know nothing at all.

'Madam, I perfectly understand that you were at that time still somewhat upset. Very good. But please to cast your mind back. Did any one of the three guests there with you, the Saint or Father Adam or Mr Dhebar, did any one of them remain with you the whole time?'

But he saw by the at once harassed look that came on to her face, by her glances from side to side as if she were a captive seeking to escape, a pursued chital deer seeking cover, that he was going to get no satisfactory answer. And he got none.

'No. No, Inspector, I cannot say. I cannot. You understand that? I really, truly cannot.'

'Yes, madam, I understand.'

And there had been nothing more he could do. Nothing more but mutter some reassurances that he was 'trying to his level best' to protect her father, to add discreetly that Sir Asif was not making his task any easier – no point in saying straight out that really the Judge himself was the enemy he had to face – and to take his leave.

To go down and continue his search for someone new to suspect, moment by moment beginning to feel that the idea of there being any such person was totally ridiculous.

And he soon realized that the opportunities at ground level for concealing an extra person in the house, someone who would be able to use a typewriter and to produce good English, were going to be small. In place of the many bedrooms on the upper floor there was down here only the

few large principal rooms and a number of other smaller
ones, and only in one of the latter would he find those signs
of occupation that he hoped for, although he did take a
careful look at the long-disused billiards room, its wide
table shrouded in a dhurry cover, the cues in their racks
delicately powdered in reddish dust.

Before long there were only the rooms underneath those
of the zenana quarter left to inspect. Before going to them,
as much to put off the moment when he had to admit
failure as anything, he decided that he ought to make sure
that the Saint and the American priest were still safely shut
away in the drawing-room.

And, besides, he might find the young American on his
own and then he could try to produce reasons why a Doctor
of Philosophy should wish to put questions to him about his
exact whereabouts earlier on in the evening.

He was, however, spared this. Both Saint and priest were
there together in the big, heavily furnished room.

They were sitting in stifled silence. No doubt the Saint's
period of self-enforced non-speaking would not end till
dawn.

The moment Father Adam spotted his head coming
round the door he leapt to his feet.

'Ganesh. Come in, man, come in. I've just been attempting
to get together a strategy on a problem I have, and I'd very
much care to hear your insights.'

'Yes?' he said apprehensively.

'Well, Ganesh, it's just this. You know, of course, about
the project of the State government here to alter the course
of the river?'

'No.'

'No? Well, I suppose shut away among your books you
don't keep up with what's going on in the real world.'

'I had certainly not heard anything of proposals to change
the course of the river right out here,' he answered, finding
he resented on behalf of all Doctors of Philosophy the
insinuation that as a class they wilfully built barriers round

themselves. 'It is the river outside that you are referring to?'

'Yes, yes. Certainly. That's the whole crux of the case. You know that centuries ago that river used to flow on a different course, right over on the other side of the house by the fort? That's why years and years ago they built that big bund out there. So's the new house wouldn't get flooded. But no sooner had they built it – hundreds and thousands of man-hours of sweated labour – than the river upped and changed its course to where it is now.'

'Well, Fath – Well, Mort, I did not at all know any of this. I have not seen very much outside the house as yet.'

'No, well, I guess not.'

'But, please, what was it you wished to ask? I am actually at this moment somewhat busy. Sir Asif's papers, you know.'

There were only those half-dozen more rooms to search. But somehow this delay had brought back his conviction that, despite all likelihood, that unknown guest was concealed in one of them. Was perhaps even at this minute attempting to obliterate all signs of his presence there before taking to another hiding-place.

'No, no, I won't keep you a minute,' Father Adam said, plainly with no intention of fulfilling the promise. 'It's just that I'd welcome a second opinion. I'd have asked Anand Baba here. What a dedicated Hindu thinks ought to carry a lot of weight. Only . . .' A look at the impassively sitting form of the Saint, legs neatly folded beneath him on the faded velvet of his chair, saffron garments lying in undisturbed folds. And a shrug.

'If it is a matter requiring the decision of a religious person I regret I do not at all qualify, Father. That is, Mort.'

'Maybe not. But you're a scholar, Doctor. A guy who's studied the great thinkers.'

The great thinkers. Did Herr Hans Gross, the fourth edition of whose classic work *Criminal Investigation* had its place of honour in his cabin back at Bombay headquarters, qualify as a great thinker? It was doubtful if Father Mort

Adam would think so.

He gave a look round the big, half-lit room hoping for inspiration. And caught the eye of the Saint. Who gave him suddenly a smile of such penetrating kindness, such all-beaming intensity, that for a little he could think of nothing else.

When he had recovered he simply asked the young American what it was that he wanted an opinion about. He would give him his view, whatever it was, whatever value it had.

'It's this, Ganesh. Sir Asif, as you know, or maybe you don't, has taken out an injunction, or whatever the ancient old legal procedure is, to stop that State government here just as they were going to breach the far end of the bund and deflect the river back on to its old course. And if that was done, you know what? It'd bring the greatest long-term benefits to hundreds of villagers out there living well below the poverty line. So, all I want to ask you is: is that right?'

All he could think of doing in face of this appallingly slanted question, about which he felt he could have no view, was to turn towards the Saint again. The first time he had voluntarily subjected himself to the power that seemed to emanate from him.

And once more he found himself receiving that smile. Later he tried to analyse it, to discover just what there was in it that had the effect it did. But he could pinpoint nothing to analyse. The flesh round the Saint's large eyes wrinkled a little so that perhaps they seemed to shine more. The mouth in his gushing, square white beard certainly moved. But hardly differently than it would have done in a grimace of pain. And yet . . . Yet he had felt, almost as if he had stepped out into the full generous heat of the sun, that he had been struck, bowled down, tumbled out of himself.

He wanted to say, 'Thank you, Babaji.' He almost did say the words out loud.

But instead he turned back to Father Adam, feeling as if he must have let the priest's question go unanswered for a full

minute, for five full minutes even, though he saw nothing in
the American's tense face – his tangly eyelashes were locked
together like the horns of two fighting deer – that showed
that the lapse of time between query and answer was anything out of the ordinary.

'Well, Mort,' he said, quite easily, 'I would certainly like
to give you my opinion. But, you know, I ought to hear Sir
Asif's side of the question also.'

The American's face fell a little.

'Yeah,' he answered. 'Yeah, I guess you've a right to do
that, Ganesh. But let me just warn you. Choose your time to
ask about it. The old boy can get pretty sore on the subject.
Pretty sore.'

He took that as a chance to make his escape. Those half-
dozen unexamined rooms scratched at his mind like a dumb
household pet tirelessly demanding entrance.

But disappointment awaited him. As all along a cold
factual voice had assured him it would. The rooms were
those that were no longer in use in the big house, indeterminate places with no obvious purpose, little more than
somewhere to put unwanted furniture. Chairs, sofas and
tables were shrouded in white sheeting, and even by the
dim light coming from the moon outside it was easy to see
that on each sheeted mound the reddish dust of the neighbourhood lay in undisturbed layers. Even the ridiculous
possibility of the person whom Sir Asif wished to hide – but
why should he wish to hide anybody? – being crouched
there holding his breath while this impertinent Inspector
from Bombay poked and pried, had to be completely dis-
counted.

And then at last he finished in the final one of the unused
rooms. There was the kitchen at the end of this passage – it
was the one with the mildew-stain map of Bangladesh on its
wall – still left unvisited, and the servants' quarter, but no
one of the typewriter-using class was going to have been put
there by Sir Asif Ibrahim. No, the hunt had come to an end,
and it had been as unsuccessful as from the start he ought to

have known it would be.

He stood at the foot of the great staircase in the hall, the
tall carved newel-post beside him, and gave a long weary
puff of a sigh, feeling defeat settle down into every crevice
of his mind.

And then, through the window on the left of the wide
double doors to the house, out in the moonlit garden, he
caught a clear glimpse of Raman. Of Raman hurrying past,
head bent, carrying in front of him a large tray draped with
a white cloth.

So there was a someone extra. Someone not hiding inside
the big old house, but concealed somewhere in its gardens.
Raman carrying out into the night what could only be a tray
of food could mean nothing else but that. And a person who
got meals taken to them by a servant was quite likely to be
someone with good English and able to use a typewriter.

Ghote felt a huge spout of hope shoot up within him. He
was going to achieve what he had been sent all this way out
here to do. He was going to find his way to the person who
had been sending death threats to Sir Asif Ibrahim. And
when he had done so he would effect an arrest.

Instantly he hurried across to the panel of brown bakelite
light switches fixed to the wall near the house door, their
wires running in an untidy clump up to the ceiling above.
Only one of the switches was in the 'On' position. He
clicked it sharply back. At once the heavy brass lantern that
illuminated the hall was extinguished.

He pulled open one of the double doors beside him,
confident now that no give-away beam of light would betray
him.

Raman was still near enough to be seen. The back of his
short white cotton jacket stood out clearly even when he
passed through the sprawling purply shadows cast by the
peaceful silver disc of the moon above. It looked as if he was
heading for the far part of the gardens, down near where the
ancient generator motor was chug-chugging away, each
time overcoming what seemed like a death choke by yet one

more minor miracle.

And, yes, this was the way that led to the old fort.

The Judge had told him its history the night before while they had been eating dinner up in the coolness of the wide flat roof. The distant black silhouette had been pointed out to him, just visible against the star-pricked blueness of the then moonless sky. It had been the original home of the family, built on a small tuft of a hill, the only one such in all the far-stretching flatness around, when centuries before they had taken the land in right of brutal conquest, spilling out from the far north, pillaging and raping. Sir Asif, most law-abiding of men, had not seemed in recounting the story to have disapproved of this as strongly as he might have done. 'Possession is nine points of the law, you know, Doctor.'

Eventually, about a hundred years ago, the rugged building had been adjudged too comfortless and the present house had been erected to replace it. But somehow the impression had been left that the fort had become a total ruin, a couple of walls only standing above heaped stones.

It was an impression, he guessed now, that he had been intended to get. The place, almost certainly, was after all at least in parts habitable.

He followed the moving shape of Raman's white jacket through the night, alternately silvery with moonlight and velvety with shadow. The chug-choke, chug-choke of the old generator engine grew louder and clearer. Areas of sweet scents came and went as his rapid steps took him past different looming overgrown shrubs, sweet cloying odours, lemony sharp odours. From away somewhere on the far side of the high-mounded useless bund, abandoned long ago by the capricious river, there came the howl of a jackal, lengthy and mournful.

It would be the moon, he thought. Jackals in his boyhood days had always howled loudest when the moon was at its brightest.

For a moment in a shadow somewhere ahead Raman's

white jacket disappeared. But it was only because he had reached the long tin shed under the soft branches of the big old tamarind tree, where the generator was chugging away, and had turned round its corner.

He quickened his pace.

He had not the least doubt now that it was to the fort that Raman was taking the substantial meal he carried.

If it was at all possible he must see exactly where he went when he had climbed the little hill.

He reached the generator shed in his turn and, pausing a moment, he swiftly tugged the knot of his necktie loose, slipped it over his head, stuffed it into his trouser pocket and whipped off his too light-coloured shirt. The trousers, thank goodness, were much darker. In the softly warm gloom now he would be much less easily seen if the Orderly did chance to turn round.

At the corner of the long tin hut he stooped and thrust the bundled shirt under a tall clump of long-dried grass. Easy enough to find it there later.

Then he hurried on.

As he had thought, the fort, when he got to the foot of the little hillock it stood on, was a good deal more substantial than Sir Asif had led him to suppose. Parts of it were certainly in ruins. But the four main walls stood massively upright, solid block on solid block of what looked in the moonlight to be pinky-red stone.

Raman, he saw, was following a path right under the walls, going round to the far side. He moved round below so as to keep him in sight. And then suddenly the white jacket disappeared into a black and narrow slit of a doorway.

No use trying to go in after him. The fellow might quite easily simply be waiting somewhere just inside. Better to watch till he came out and then attempt to make contact with whoever it was in there who had volunteered, probably just for the length of his own stay here, to live down in this remote corner of the gardens.

He stood where he was, confident that bare-chested he

would be invisible to the Orderly whenever he emerged again, and strained to hear the least tell-tale sound from inside the fort. Certainly Raman seemed to be taking his time. He had already been a good deal longer than would be needed just to put down the tray with its load of dishes, to salaam and leave. Was he keeping this mysterious person in touch with events in the house? 'The Doctor from Bombay spoke with Judge sahib for half an hour tonight. I do not know what they said, but Judge sahib was very-very angry after.'

Or would it be a very different kind of report that was being made? 'Yes, sahib, I was leaving the note you had written on your typewriter for Judge sahib to find, as you told. And the Doctor from Bombay saw. Sahib, I do not trust this man.'

In the soft darkness a heavy beetle whirred its way close past his head.

No, Raman would not have been saying that. He was too much the Judge's man to have lent himself to any enemy. Twenty-four hours of seeing master and servant together had been enough to have made that plain beyond doubt. Raman – had he not been in the Judge's service for more than thirty years? – was devoted to the old man. Look at the way he quietly accepted those outbursts of rage. The Judge could say anything to him, it seemed. No insult exceeded the bounds of his happy patience. It was re-markable even that he had gone so far as to have offered the Judge his notice, if that was what one of the old man's rage-shouted remarks had meant earlier on. No, it was quite clear: Raman could be in no way an accessary to anyone issuing threats against Sir Asif.

So he must then be Sir Asif's agent, coming out here to bring food to whoever it was that the Judge wanted to keep out of his own way. For whatever reason.

Suddenly in the narrow, deep black slit in the reddish walls of the fort a white shape appeared. Raman in his white jacket, with the empty tray and its cloth now held carelessly at his side.

He drew back deeper into the bush that hid him.

But the Judge's faithful servant walked past him in complete unconcern, humming quietly to himself what sounded like some old boatman's song from the South, a regular rhythm like the steady dipping of a paddle.

CHAPTER VII

HE LET FIVE minutes go by, measured by counting to himself steadily under his breath. And then he ventured to move. Alert for the smallest unexpected sound, he climbed up the little hill and made his way carefully round the massive walls of the ruin. It was not difficult to find the black slit of a doorway where Raman had disappeared.

He peeped in. It was just possible to make out a flight of steps leading sharply downwards.

So the habitable parts of the fort were underground. It was likely enough. Places of this sort were always built with underground rooms in them, to hide treasure, to keep safe prisoners, to protect powder for the cannon.

Cautiously he felt his way down first one deep step and then another. He paused a moment. Still no sound and ahead only inky blackness.

Then, as carefully, he felt his way down further, step by step. He had counted twelve of them, enough to have brought him well below the level of the ground of the fort itself, before his exploring foot told him that there was a flat floor in front of him.

A stickily choking odour came into his nostrils. Bats. It was the smell of bats' droppings deposited here year after year after year.

Had Raman really penetrated this far into the darkness? Endured this much stink? He must have done. There was nowhere else to go but onwards.

With arms spread out in front of him till his fingertips were touching the tacky walls to either side, he advanced step by gliding step. And then, after perhaps six or seven yards, there came a sharp right-angled turn and, as soon as he had negotiated it, there ahead at some distance he saw a faint light.

Should he call out? No, better to gain the advantage of surprise over whoever it was living down here. And with that advantage, to get out of them, perhaps in a few minutes only, why it was that they were threatening the life of the old Judge.

He might even at any moment begin to hear in this bat-stinking darkness the tap-tap-tap of a typewriter.

Thanks to the dim glow of light ahead, he was able to move forward along the new passageway – it was as narrow as the first – at a slightly better speed. And a few yards further down it a new fact became apparent to him. At the far end, where the light came apparently from round another sharp corner, there were bars, iron bars, shutting off the entire height of the passageway like those of a lock-up in some police station back in Bombay.

Still moving soundlessly as he could in his shoes, he glided onwards until he had come right up to the bars. They formed, he was able to make out, a gate with a heavy lock in it and behind them there was a stone ledge in the wall forming a narrow table on which there now rested three broad green banana-leaves, each with neat heaps of food on it.

Plainly Raman had just put them there. But a meal to be eaten off banana leaves as if it was some village repast, yet served to whoever was here by the Judge's own Orderly? It did not add up.

He gave the barred door in front of him a cautious tug. It was firmly locked.

A prisoner then? Some person imprisoned down here? But why? Had the Judge in his old age gone mad and begun to administer his own justice? Sentencing those who had infringed his strict moral code to so many years in his private gaol? But who? Who would he have found for this extraordinary punishment?

He stood beside the barred gate feeling the questions spring up and flutter furiously in his mind as if they were the very bats hanging above him parting in panic from their resting places.

In the silence then he began to make out one tiny insistent sound. Water, or some other liquid, drip-drip-dripping somewhere on the far side.

The barely discernible sound, the smeary stink of the bat droppings, the darkness behind and the faint light in front: there was nothing else.

And then, with complete suddenness, into that quiet and stillness there came a raging blast of noise.

It was a scream.

It was a roar.

It was a wild on-hurtling rush.

And there in an instant, not a yard away on the opposite side of the barred gate, was a man. A wild, powerful caricature of a man, bare chest like a boulder, shoulders like two heaving, thrusting pistons, a head that was all savagery, beard jutting out at every angle, leaving only two rolling eyes and a small triangle of compressed nose to be seen, and the open mouth glinting with fierce, canine teeth. The noise, the deafening roaring, was issuing from that, like steam issuing from some torn split in the rock-bound earth.

Two huge hands had seized the bars of the gate, and with force enough, it seemed, to tear the whole thing from the ancient hewn stones in which it was embedded, they were shaking it like an enraged gorilla in a zoo.

And those rolling uncontrolled eyes were conscious of him, there in the darkness back where he had stepped.

Then from the welter of noise there emerged words. Words in shouted but recognizable English.

'Spy. Traitor. Damned spy. British lover. Spy. Spy.

Traitor. Traitor. Traitor.'

It raged on. But at last slackened, if only for an instant or two.

He leapt in. 'Please. Who are you? Who are you?'

The sharpness he had infused into his voice had an immediate effect on the lunging elemental creature on the far side of the bars. His screaming abruptly stopped and he stood glaring in sudden silence.

Glaring, it came to him in an almost ridiculous sidestep of the mind, with a force parallel to nothing other than the smile of the Saint, the smile he had experienced not so long before in the faded civilization of the ornate drawing-room of the big old house.

He was so taken aback by this involuntary association that for several moments it did not occur to him to take advantage of the sudden silence to repeat his question to the man crouching facing him. Then he became abruptly aware of the spicy odour of the food on the four broad banana leaves on the far side of the bars, a tickling of the nostrils, and he collected himself together.

'Please tell me who it is you are?'

The boulder-chested man glared back at him. But then at last he produced not a direct answer but some coherent words.

'The British. They have planned this. They know that if Sikander Ibrahim is free their raj will end in blood. They know that, the swine. In blood. In blood. In blood.'

The voice rose to a throbbing scream again, and once more the bars of the door were rattled till it seemed the whole affair would come heaving from the stonework.

But there was no need now to try the effect of another sharply put question. He had learnt, he realized, what he needed to know.

The name the wild creature had given himself, to begin with. Sikander Ibrahim. That and one characteristic feature of that convulsed, bearded face had told him that here kept behind bars underground in this ruined old fort was, surely, Sir Asif Ibrahim's own son down to his very squashed-in nose.

And it was plain too, plain beyond any possible mitigation, that Sikander Ibrahim was mad. He was living in a state where no bounds of any sort controlled him. And he was living, too, in a past that had long gone.

The Judge's secret. He had penetrated it.

No wonder Sir Asif had not welcomed the arrival of an inspector of police in his house when there could be no doubt that his son should not be here in private hands but kept in the assured safety of a proper asylum for the violently insane.

So what was he going to do with his piece of knowledge he had gained?

The answer came to him even as he posed the question. He was going to make use of it. Quite wrong not to make immediate arrangements to have this illegally kept lunatic transferred to the appropriate State institution. But the threat of being able to do that had at last put into his hands a really powerful lever with which to move the old immovable Judge.

Because one thing seemed clear: those carefully typewritten notes could not possibly have come from the raging maniac on the far side of the bars down here. Even in the highly unlikely case of him being able to leave this prison, he would never creep anywhere. If he got out he would surely rage and destroy and perhaps even slaughter.

So, for the Judge's own good, he must make the fullest use of this weapon he had been lucky enough – or, no, be just to himself: not just lucky, persistent enough too – to get into his hands. He must use it to blackmail Sir Asif. There was no other way of putting it. There was no other course of action open to him. He must blackmail the just Judge.

CHAPTER VIII

BACK IN THE HOUSE, rescued shirt once more on his back, though crumpled and more than a little earth-stained, Ghote found that it was already the hour for the next stage in the slow unvarying routine of the establishment's life. It was 'Drinks Before Dinner' time.

He had experienced the ritual the night before and had not liked it. He had been offered whisky and soda, nothing else, and had declined. So too had that then almost totally incomprehensible figure, the robeless American priest, a refusal which temporarily made him seem more likely. Until almost at once remarks had come from his lips which, to his mind, could be called nothing other than 'sheer Naxalitism', the young American rivalling even India's most extreme Leftists in the extravagance of his denunciations of contemporary power structures. The Saint, on that occasion, had not even been approached by Raman with his silver tray and array of cut-glass tumblers, whisky bottle and soda jug. Nor had Begum Roshan.

So 'Drinks Before Dinner' had consisted of the four of them sitting in the big faded drawing-room, its air still torpid from the day's heat despite the rose-water which the servants had flung against the chick blinds, watching Sir Asif sip his way slowly through two long tumblers of indolently bubbling liquid while they batted to and fro occasional insipid remarks.

Then he had not at all known what a Doctor of Philosophy ought to be saying in such circumstances. Twenty-four hours later he was no better informed.

But now he dreaded the occasion a good deal more. Because at some time during it – the evening before it had lasted a full hour – he would have to ask the Judge to give him yet one more private interview. And if necessary, if the unbending old man refused to grant his request, as it was most likely that he would, then matters would have to be taken a stage further and he would have to hint plainly at the power he now had with which to enforce his wish.

But having the power was not going to make it any easier to use. That he knew.

And he was already a little late. No time, damn it, to put on another shirt. He tried brushing at the reddish earth marks with the tips of his fingers. It was not a success.

Hurry along the now more familiar high-ceilinged passage – yes, no bluish map-of-Bangladesh mildew stain on the wall – and open the door.

'Ah, Doctor Ghote. We were awaiting you.'

The Judge was sitting, back formidably upright, white pagri stiff above his head, both veined hands resting on the knob of his stick, in one of the tall faded velvet chairs exactly facing the doorway. And a yard or so away stood Raman holding out his silver tray with its crystal-shining tumblers, whisky bottle and soda jug and looking distinctly puzzled.

At once he realized what the situation was. The Judge had ordered Raman not to begin serving the drinks until all the guests were assembled, not in fact to give him his own drink, since none of the others seemed to take whisky, until this missing intrusive newcomer was present. But the exact moment when 'Drinks Before Dinner' were served was customarily sacrosanct. Poor Raman. A fearful dilemma put in front of him. And, no doubt, in telling him not to come forward with his tray the Judge had been as fiercely scathing as ever.

Well, at least the fellow was used to such fury.

Even the others, he saw as he offered a stammered apology, were looking uneasily embarrassed. Or Begum Roshan and Father Adam were. Because the Saint, sitting with heels tucked neatly under himself on the soft velvet of his chair, was gazing in the direction of one of the room's tall carved wooden screens with a look of far serenity on his gushingly white-bearded face.

He found himself hoping hard that that unseeing gaze would turn towards himself and that he would be subjected once more to one of those smiles, even though he felt at the same time that if he were to receive a smile it would somehow show to all the others that this was the man who not long before had been creeping through the gardens outside doing the work of a spy.

He frowned. Surely he had been right to have done what he had? How else could he now save the Judge from himself? Save, in all likelihood, the old man's life?

He turned away sharply and made his way over to sit in a vacant chair, holding his head a little stiffly so as to avoid seeing the saffron-robed figure of the Saint.

'Raman, offer Doctor Ghote some whisky. Don't just stand there looking like an idiot.'

Sir Asif seemed to be in fine form. How deeply buried again was the man who had once set free a certain Vaishnavite singer of holy songs and had learnt later that he had killed again?

And before long it would be his task to put before this stone figure a demand for yet another interview.

'Raman, Doctor Ghote appears to have been lying down on the earth somewhere. His shirt is stained. Go and fetch a brush. No, no, man, my drink must wait. There are some laws of hospitality still, little though they seem to be regarded nowadays.'

Raman produced his sudden horseshoe grin, quickly set down his tray and hurried towards the door.

'No, no. No, please. Kindly not to bother. I cannot think how I was getting my shirt in this disgraceful state, but please do not trouble yourselves about it.'

'My dear Doctor, we must trouble ourselves. We cannot help seeing the curious garment. We know no gentleman would wish to appear at dinner in that state.'

'Yes. No. No, of course, Sir Asif. But – but please may I leave and put on another shirt? And, please, do please have your whisky.'

'It is good of you, Ghote, to concern yourself so much with my comforts. And perhaps you had better leave us. Poor Raman is quite confused by all this.'

He shot up from his chair, saw that – damn, damn – some of the earth from his shirt had left a stain on the pallid velvet padding of one of its arms, stooped to brush it off, decided that doing so would only draw attention to the mess, turned, looked round the long room and caught, full on him like a searchlight beam directed from a heavy-duty lamp manned by a full Army unit, the Saint's smile.

He stood still, conscious with one part of his mind that he must look like a fool with mouth hanging open and a stare of pure stupidity in his eyes, but incapable of moving and even determined not to move.

At last – Had two seconds only passed? Had ten minutes? – he broke away, got himself over to the door and fumbled with its knob and found himself eventually out in the tall, dimly-lit passage.

He moved off slowly down it, thoughts tumbling in his mind.

The Saint. Did he really have the extraordinary power he seemed to possess? Or was it just that he had the trick of hypnosis and he himself, cut off in this remote place, was unusually susceptible?

And what about the other three possible suspects whom he hoped to find out about when he had blackmailed Sir Asif into telling all he knew? Which of them, now that the someone extra was no longer a possibility, was in fact the person threatening the Judge? Determined, boring-in Mr Dhebar? Or Father Adam, that Naxalite? Or was it possible after all that the whole business was simply some obscure notion of Begum Roshan's. That she wanted, not to kill her father, but to frighten him, and that when this had seemed not to be effective she had gone to a little trouble to make the notes she had written public knowledge so as to increase that pressure?

Unless she did want to kill her father. And was trying to

create for herself a kind of alibi in advance.

But until he knew more of Sir Asif's relations with all of them – Why, he still had no idea what an American priest with Naxalite opinions was doing in this house, or why it was that the Saint chose to come here to sleep his nights on the floor of that little-used musty room – he would get no further. No, his interview ahead with the Judge was the key to it all. And the moment when he must persuade that obstinate, just man to give him that interview.

And if he lacked courage to demand that, then before long the slow dying atmosphere of the place would envelop him as it seemed to have enveloped them all and turn him into another remote ghost-like figure gliding to and fro within it.

Shirt. Shirt. Shirt.

He raced the rest of the way to his room, tugged open the door of the almirah, pulled out a shirt, inspected it, decided it looked all right, wondered whether a servant would see to taking away the one he was peeling off and handing it to the dhobi for washing, tugged his way into the fresh garment, carefully re-knotted his tie and started down again for the big furniture-crowded faded drawing-room. And the prospect of tackling Sir Asif.

Talk, when he re-entered the big dim room, seemed to have eddied once again to a standstill. Sir Asif looked at him gravely and took a sip from his glass. He appeared to have got through only a third of his first tumblerful. It was going to be a good long time before he had little by little finished his quota of two.

But, though then a mercifully long period seemed to lie ahead before he had to put his pistol to the Judge's head, he found himself suddenly determined to make the move now. The bubble of indecision in which they all seemed to be floating had abruptly become offensive to him. He would pierce it. Now.

'Sir Asif,' he said with grating briskness, 'it occurred to me while I was up in my room that really there are still a great many unanswered questions. About the matter we discussed earlier.'

The Judge said nothing. But the coldly fixed expression on that face with the curiously flattened nose – the nose he shared with his son, his mad concealed son – gave all the answer anyone could have wanted.

He braced himself again.

'So, sir, perhaps it would be convenient if we had a short meeting in the library before it is time for dinner tonight?'

Again Sir Asif did not speak.

But his eyes said: Young man, you have suggested altering the established practice of my house. It has been the custom for drinks to be taken before dinner in here for year upon year. Never has anyone at any time left this room before the hour of dinner. Now you have dared to suggest that someone should.

The silence lengthened.

He wondered for a sweat-flushing moment whether he should turn to the Saint, beg from him another warming wave of reassurance.

But, no, he would fight this battle on his own. He had to. The Saint would not give his blessing to blackmail. And he would know that blackmail was precisely what was taking place at this moment. He would know it.

He coughed. A grating sound. 'Sir, I hope my suggestion is not upsetting.' He was having to expel each separate word as if each was a shot from a revolver. 'But, sir, I am not at all clear concerning your family bio-data. And I can hardly assist with your Memoirs, sir, without knowing about your own family.'

He felt obliged then to give a light laugh by way of covering up what to Sir Asif ought to have been a plain message. And, combined with those remarked-upon signs of his having recently been prowling round the gardens of the house, a clear threat.

In the big room – the light from its single chandelier was so dim and orangey that it was hardly possible to see into the far corner by the photograph-crammed piano – the curious sound he had produced fell away to nothingness.

He stood waiting. Perhaps soon Sir Asif would join in this pretence of a conversation, and by conniving at the pretence acknowledge that a message had been conveyed to him.

In a few moments he even began to hope that one of the others would say something that would break the increasingly oppressive silence. The Saint, of course, was excused. But generally Begum Roshan was concerned to keep some sort of conversation going when they were all together like this. But she was making no effort to do so now. Simply sitting there in her high-backed chair, her long fingers, thin to the bone, plucking at one edge of her sari, lifting it and letting it drop, lifting it again and letting it drop once more. And Father Adam, Mort, why was he not finding some chink in which to insert his appalling Naxalite views? But he was sitting in blank silence. Had Sir Asif said something while he had been out changing his shirt that had reduced them both to furious silence? As likely as not he had.

Well, he would have to say something himself, something more. And he would do it. He would go on until he had presented Sir Asif beyond any possibility of misunderstanding with his ultimatum. 'Grant me another private talk, and this time tell me everything I need to know. Or. Or I will see that your insane son is transferred to some State institution and that all the world knows about it.'

He cleared his throat and took a step forward to ensure that the maximum of the grudging light from the big chandelier fell on him.

'Sir Asif,' he said, 'it was in considering the parts of your Memoirs that deal with your earlier days that this query arose in my mind. Sir Asif, am I not right to think that some fifty years ago a son was born to you?'

In the old man's eyes he saw a glare of anger mounting. At any instant, he felt, it would spill out in such a fire-blast of rage as poor Raman was accustomed to endure. Would he take it as unflinchingly as the Orderly?

Or perhaps he would not have to. Perhaps instead it

would be clear that his duty would be not to bend before the
fire-storm but to battle it. To answer taunt with hard
allegation.

Because, whichever way was necessary, he must obtain the
Judge's co-operation. Otherwise the chances of him stopping the old man's murder were slim indeed.

But Sir Asif was trying the tactic of silence still, suppressing
the anger that so plainly boiled volcano-like just beneath the
surface.

'Sir Asif?' he asked again, with as much sharpness as if he
was livening up some reluctant witness from the squalor of
the Bombay chawls.

'Yes. Fifty years ago a son was born to me.'

He softened at once with the admission obtained. 'Yes,
yes, Sir Asif. And it was what should be said in the Memoirs
concerning this son that I wanted to discuss. And various
other matters also.'

The Judge's face showed no sign, however, of yielding one
quarter-inch more. But the 'Out of Bounds' declaration,
when it came, was not put up by him but by his daughter.

She shot from her chair, face quivering in tiny whirlpools
of uncontrollable muscular movement.

'No, Doctor Ghote. You are not to speak of Sikander.
You are to leave him out of account altogether. In whatever
you do. He does not exist. Not for you. Not at all.'

As suddenly as she had risen up out of her chair to stand,
a taut strip of sprung steel, and deliver her veto, she
collapsed back into it.

Her father turned towards her.

'Roshan, how often have I told you that when I require
assistance from you I shall ask?'

And then he once more confronted his adversary.

In the set face with its squashed-down nose he saw no
indication yet of surrender. But the old man had yielded to the
point of admitting that he had a son. So press him, press
him. And to hell with any pretence of being only the dutiful
assistant sent to help with the Memoirs.

'Sir Asif, the future of your son is in question. Can we go now to discuss?'

But there was not the tiniest softening in the ivory-hard face.

'No, Doctor, we cannot go now – to discuss. There is no room for discussion of this or any other matter.'

And now the rage began to issue from the volcano. Not in the great spewing roar he had half expected but in small, still contained jets.

'Doctor, I made my position perfectly clear to you earlier this evening. I had some obligations to you. Excessively small obligations. And in no circumstances did I intend to venture one step beyond them. But now you have had the impertinence to pry into my private affairs, and unless I am much mistaken you are threatening to use the knowledge you have gained as my guest here to place me in a position that you think will embarrass or even shame me. Well, learn that with that I consider any obligations that I had have now come to an end. You will kindly leave my house.'

Perversely what he chiefly felt after the battering was admiration. Sir Asif had acted as he himself would have liked to have acted in the same circumstances. In the altogether unlikely event of circumstances of any similarity ever occurring in his own modest life. To stick to a principle, even one that was absurd, although sticking to it meant that a secret you had guarded with enormous care and at great expense over long years was exposed to the world: that was fine. Fine.

But it was also damnable.

It broke his last frail link with the only source of information that would enable him to do the task he had been sent there to do, to save the Judge's life. And there was nothing now he could do to restore that link. In due course he could put in a report which would eventually result in a police detachment presenting itself here at the old house and escorting Sikander Ibrahim to a State mental asylum. And that would cause great distress to Sir Asif. But it would be no more than an empty revenge.

The Judge had won. Won, even if in winning he had perhaps put his life at yet greater risk. But there was nothing to be done but accept that victory.

'Very well, sir,' he said, 'since you ask I will go.'

And he turned and walked out of the big dimly-lit furniture-crowded room with what dignity he could muster.

It was a very long way to the door.

CHAPTER IX

UP IN THE SANCTUARY of the room that had been his, Ghote sat on the edge of the high hard bed, the old fan silent above him, and contemplated his position. It was a depressing process.

Here he was, the thin end of the Deputy Commissioner's wedge, an instrument placed in position with the sole object of penetrating little by little the wooden obstinacy of old Sir Asif. And the wedge had been snapped clean off. It had been up to him not only to save Sir Asif's life by identifying the sender of those threatening notes, but, as important perhaps to the Deputy Commissioner, to forestall the avalanche of trouble that would descend if the Judge was murdered and his influential cousin, the MLA, told the world that the Bombay CID had been clearly warned of what might happen.

And he had put himself beyond being able to do anything.

There was no possibility of his staying on in the house. That was certain. He had no shadow of right to be here. He was, as Sir Asif had so scathingly pointed out, a guest. Sir Asif's own guest. And, no getting past it, he had abused Sir Asif's hospitality. The fact that he had done so in order to save the old man from himself did not really put his action in any better a light.

No, he would have to go. And as soon as maybe.

But thinking now what he would actually have to do to leave sent his level of depression down another thick layer. How was he going to get away? The town was miles and miles distant. It was already night. Even if he walked all the way to the village, and there was the river to get over before he did that, full of hazards shrunken though it was, he would never persuade some villager after darkness had fallen to let him sleep on the platform outside his hut or succeed in inducing the owner of a bullock-cart to take him on to the town and its railway station. Why, they would scarcely get there before dawn. And the village dogs. What would he have to face from them, arriving there a stranger and at night?

He slipped from the bed and began, because he felt that it was the least he ought to do, to collect together his clothes and other possessions before packing them in the solitary suitcase he had brought with him, a bulky old cardboardy affair in a bright and unlikely shade of tan, of which he had felt decidedly ashamed under Raman's gaze when he had arrived. He put various items into the case and then took them out again when he realized that they ought not to get crushed by the heavier things he had left out, or back at home – how far away that seemed: how different a life – Protima would draw the line at having to iron again shirts she had already ironed in anticipation of his visit to the distinguished Judge, Sir Asif Ibrahim. Then he was interrupted by a sharp knock on the door.

'Come in,' he called, wondering whether it was a servant returning the dirty shirt that had already been taken to the dhobi.

It was not. It was Begum Roshan.

'Inspector Ghote,' she said, coming in quickly and closing the heavy door behind her. 'There is no need any longer, I suppose, for the pretence of "Doctor". Inspector, I have come to discuss what can be done. Once again my father has gone too far.'

'I am afraid, madam, that that was altogether my fault. I

had hoped to force Sir Asif into a position where he would
give me maximum co-operation. I should have known
that he is not a man who can be forced when he has made up
his mind that he is in the right.'

'My father is a man who cannot be forced ever,' Begum
Roshan replied, clenching up the edge of her sari for an
instant in tautly nervous fingers. 'God knows, in my life
how often I have tried.'

'But, madam, then there is nothing to be done. Sir Asif
has said I am unwelcome in his house. I am his guest. I
must go.'

'And when you go, then what?' Begum Roshan asked
wildly. 'You report that we are keeping a dangerous madman
here and, because there are people in the town who would
like nothing better than to humiliate Sir Asif Ibrahim, a
force of Armed Police comes out here, accompanied no
doubt by the town photographer, and they drag Sikander
back with them to some disgusting hole that they claim is
safer for him. That is it, isn't it? Isn't it?'

He looked down at his feet. 'Madam, you would not deny
that Mr Sikander Ibrahim is a dangerous person. Think of
the bars that are necessary to keep him confined there in the
fort.'

'Bars?' Begum Roshan said fiercely. 'Are there bars? I
never visit Sikander, Inspector. None of us does. It makes
him worse. But if you tell me there are bars, there are bars.'

She turned away, looked round the bare room as if seeking
some support, and at last sank heavily on to the edge of the
bed.

A pile of his neatly rolled socks tumbled to the floor. He
moved to pick them up, but then thought that to do so
would seem to show a lack of concern for his visitor's
troubles.

'Madam,' he said. 'Madam, I very well appreciate your
earnest desire to keep Mr Sikander Ibrahim within the
bounds of the family property. He is after all your brother.
But nevertheless, madam, it is contrary to the law to harbour

an individual considered dangerous. And I am a police officer, madam.'

Begum Roshan's head was turned away, looking down at the white bedcover and at a single pair of socks, his brown ones, that had rolled in a different direction from their fellows.

He heard her give a choked sob.

'Madam, I must do my duty. A police officer cannot refrain from that just because he is having to cause some hardship.'

Begum Roshan made an impatient movement with her hand. A long fingernail just flicked the brown socks and moved them about an inch.

Her next sob was louder.

'Please, madam, consider what your father himself would do in my circumstances. He would not give in. You know that he would not.'

Now she looked up at him. A tic was working in her right cheek.

'Inspector, if Sikander is taken away it is the end for me. I cannot endure seeing my father's humiliation. It will be the end. The end. Do you understand? There is a limit beyond which I cannot go.'

He sighed. 'But please to think. The secret of Mr Sikander is out now. I know. Sooner or later he will have to be transferred to some official place of restraint. I cannot alter that.'

She was still looking at him, her large eyes glistening with tears.

'Sooner, Inspector?' she said. 'Or later? Inspector, you do not have to report Sikander's presence here tonight.'

He bit at the inside of his lower lip in hesitation.

'No,' he agreed at last. 'No, it would be carrying duty beyond a sensible point if I were to insist on passing on the information that has come to my knowledge within minutes, or hours even, of having acquired it.'

Begum Roshan slowly straightened her back and took a

deep breath. The brown socks rolled a few inches more, reached the bed's edge and dropped down to join their fellows.

He thought that now it would be all right to gather them all up.

'In any case,' he said, stooping, 'I am not at all certain how I am to get away. So no question of reporting at present arises.'

'No, Inspector.' Abruptly Begum Roshan was all taut spring again. 'No, no, no. That is one thing certain. You are not going to leave this house. You are needed here. Here you must stay. You shall not go.'

'But, madam, what to do?'

Her large eyes were flashing defiance now.

'I shall think of something,' she announced. 'He will not trample over me this time. He has to be protected. He must not be allowed to sacrifice his life for a whim.'

'But, madam, is it a whim only?' he asked, felt bound to ask, the thought of Sir Asif's considered determination strong in his mind.

'Well, what else is it but a whim? He must well realize that a policeman cannot act in a case when he knows nothing. That is just common sense. And he knows so much about the people he has allowed into his house. He knows what a devil that Father Adam is. The man was sent to us through our cousin who is in the Pakistani Embassy in Washington. He would have told my father all about him.'

'What would he have told?' he asked, pleased to have at last learnt just a little about the Naxalite priest, even though it was now too late.

Begum Roshan flung out her thin-fleshed hands in a gesture of exasperation.

'How should I know what he was told?' she demanded. 'I am the last to hear anything. Nothing, nothing is ever said to me. He comes one day and says he has had a letter from Cousin Karim in Washington and that there be a Christian priest coming who has been sent to India to do

social work in some jungly area and who is now ill. Of course
he is ill. And he is bad also, but because he is a friend of
Cousin Karim, Cousin Karim whom we have not even seen
since Partition, since he was just a small boy, then that man
must be welcomed here. It is impossible. Impossible.'

'But if Sir Asif knew of these subversive views before
Father Adam came,' he asked, 'would he not have ascertained
whether there was any real danger?'

'No, no. That was not necessary. Those opinions were
nothing. Until there came that terrible quarrel over blasting
the bund.'

'That was the question of altering the course of the river?
They were going to employ explosives for that?'

'Yes, yes. Of course my father was perfectly right to go to
law to prevent it happening. And he did so at the last
moment only, too. He was perfectly right in that.'

'But,' he ventured, 'from what Father Adam told me
there appeared to be advantages in the scheme.'

'Nonsense, nonsense. For hundreds of years the family
has cared for the poor here. The villagers are Hindu, we
are Muslim. But we have looked after them. Like fathers.
It was our duty. And then along come these people with their
plans and their forecasts and tell us that the river must
flow between the house and the fort so that more fields can
be irrigated. What appalling nonsense.'

He decided that he had gone quite far enough in voicing
the other side of the argument. It would be no use crossing
such an emotional person as Begum Roshan. Emotional and
confused. What was her real attitude towards her father?
Did she herself even know? With one breath she had
denounced him as a tyrant, with the next she had plainly
showed that she worshipped him.

No, keep well clear. There were some frontiers it was
sheer folly to cross.

'Yes, yes,' he murmured. 'It is all most difficult. Most.'

The soft tone seemed to satisfy her.

'Every girl in the village has always received the gift of

a new sari on her marriage,' she declared, carried away by her determination to vindicate her father. 'When any one of them is ill, medicine is sent. Where there has been a drought, lakhs and lakhs of rupees have been paid out.'

He thought. Clearly Sir Asif had been determined that the course of the river should not be changed. And probably too his decision had been taken from the best of motives, and not with the thought in mind of the risky prisoner under the old fort. But for whatever reasons he had opposed the scheme, he would have been adamant in his objections. And Father Adam? Was the man not a complete hothead, revealed as such in everything he uttered?

So here was a possible motive for sending those threats, and even for committing murder if they did not achieve their purpose, with the hints about the Madurai Trial no more than something designed to confuse.

But now it was surely too late for him to do anything about it.

'Madam,' he said to Begum Roshan, 'allow me to assure you that immediately on return to Bombay I will have the fullest inquiries made about Father Adam. If he is a danger-ous anti-social, then he can be expelled from the country.'

She looked at him with scorn. 'And how long will that take, Inspector? We have only twelve days, hardly twelve now.'

'Well, madam, that might be time enough. I will work to my level best to speed up the process.'

Yet securing the expulsion of a foreigner about whom at this moment nothing detrimental was known would not be easy. And to do so in the time remaining would be yet more difficult.

Even if Father Adam was the person threatening the Judge.

'No, Inspector, that is not good enough.'

Begum Roshan strode across to the window and gazed passionately into the velvet darkness as if out there waiting was an answer to the impossible.

And it seemed a moment later that from the formless night she had found one. She wheeled round.

'Yes. Yes, that is what we must do.'

He felt anger race across his mind in a thunder of hooves. The stupid woman. With her great declarations that this must be done or that must be done or it would be the end of the world. Why was she incapable of realizing that sometimes there was nothing to be done but accept the facts? Why did she have to go about all the time taking such stands?

And what had she got into her head now?

'Yes, madam?'

'This is what we will do. I will call Raman at once and he will take the motor-car and drive you into the town, to the railway-station. There you will say goodbye to him. But as soon as the car has gone you will walk to the office of *The Sputnik* where Mr Dhebar resides. I will draw you a plan of the way there. Now, if you tell him that I sent you, he will let you stay there for the night – he will always do what I ask, I do not know why – and then early in the morning you can borrow his motor-scooter and come back here. By that time the watchman will have left the gardens and you can hide there.'

Objections had been springing up in his mind like targets at a shooting booth. At last he got an opportunity to voice one.

'But – but I very much regret, it would be quite impossible to hide in the gardens. Where would I go?'

'Oh, nonsense, nonsense. There are all sorts of places. There is the generator shed. That would do very well. None of the servants except Raman goes near there. We have told them the fort is haunted. It keeps them away from Sikander.'

'But Raman will find me there and tell Sir Asif.'

Begum Roshan drew herself up. She was a ranee of old, commanding troops. 'You must not let Raman find you. It should not be difficult. He only goes to the shed once every evening, to start the engine. He puts in just enough fuel to last till midnight, and that is that. You can keep out of his way that long.'

It was plain that he could. But he was reluctant to admit it. Begum Roshan's high commanding tone was infuriating. He offered another objection.

'But even if I can hide in the gardens, how would I be able, so far from the house, to find out who is sending Sir Asif those notes?'

Begum Roshan waved a thin, long-fingered hand.

'Oh, you will be able to do something. You can come into the house in the afternoons when everyone is sleeping, and you can protect my father if it comes to the last day. That man has said he will not strike till the anniversary of the Madurai sentences.'

'Yes, that is all very well, but – '

'No, Inspector. You must do this. You must. I will not hear of any objections.'

And before he could put any more, she had swept out, fine chiffon sari swirling behind her in the thick, hot air.

CHAPTER X

GHOTE FOLLOWED the white-jacketed form of Raman through the gardens and their succession of night scents, sweet and heavy or lemony fragrant, down towards the river and the road. The moon had sunk beneath the black outline of the old useless bund and following the path required concentration, despite the large oil-lantern the Orderly was carrying.

What was he going to do? He found it hard to make up his mind. Was he going to fall in with Begum Roshan's absurd idea and return to lurk in the generator shed attempting to continue his task by remote control? Or was he going to accept his dismissal at Sir Asif's hands, go back to

Bombay and report unsuccess?

He hardly liked the prospect of that. But if the Judge had rescinded his agreement to have a police officer in his house that was what he had done, and it would be unreasonable to insist on guarding him when he was adamant in refusing any protection at all. Yet to be chased away . . . It hurt.

So was Begum Roshan's plan so ridiculous after all? It had been the slender prospect it offered of being able to stand by his given duty that had made him in the end stifle all the objections he had had and allow her to give Raman instructions to drive him to the town. But presenting himself at the offices of *The Sputnik* and suggesting borrowing its editor's scooter, just like that? He was by no means sure he saw himself doing it.

Ahead, Raman, that bulky tan suitcase balanced easily on his head, came to a halt.

'Sahib will want to take off his shoes,' he said.

They were at the river's edge.

He lowered himself to the dry powdery ground and tugged off one shoe and then the other, one sock and then the next.

'Ready.'

There had been no conversation between them as they had made their way through the gardens. He felt that Raman was looking on himself as Sir Asif's actual representative. Seeing this unwelcome guest off the premises.

Sir Asif, of course, had been conspicuously absent when he had left. He would be shut up in the library, no doubt, and there would be no sudden glint from a lifted curtain as he had begun his march back to where he had come from, no face under stiffly wound white pagri peering even for the briefest of moments. No, the old man would be sitting in his customary chair beside the inlaid-ivory table, the lamp shining on the pages of some volume of Urdu poetry. He would disdain to give the guest who had broken the rules one single thought more.

Raman held the lantern higher and they stepped down on to the river bed. It was hard to keep a safe footing. The water, when at last they had to wade for a few yards, felt warm round his calves.

On the far side the Orderly halted once more while he put socks and shoes on again.

He would have liked to have left them off. The heat-powdered earth was soft under his feet. But he knew that he was still expected to behave like a burra sahib: he had been under Sir Asif's roof, had sat with him at table.

From a clump of scrubby trees nearby came the sudden harsh cry of a kokila bird, disturbed perhaps by the light of the lantern.

'Sahib is ready?'

'Yes, ready.'

It was not a long walk to the padlocked hut where Sir Asif's car was kept, a tin building not unlike the generator hut. Raman set down the suitcase – did he despise it? – and hauled back the corrugated iron doors. They screeched abominably.

Inside, the lantern's grimy rays showed a truly magnificent car. It was not possible to see it down to the last detail. It was too much covered with dust and with the webs of long-undisturbed spiders. But there was a radiator grille of solid silvery metal, a long bonnet behind it and a low canvas hood behind that. And beside the driver's seat a rubber horn bulb.

Was it a Rolls-Royce? He thought not. There ought to be a little goddess on the top of the radiator for that, surely. No, it might be a Bentley. Or had there been something once called a Daimler? Whatever it was, it looked as if it too dated back to the days of the Madurai Conspiracy Case. A relic of a forgotten past.

'This way, sahib.'

Raman held the lantern high and preceded him to the rear of the ancient vehicle, where he ceremoniously opened a door for him.

There was the little curled-up body of a dead gecko on the broad leather seat. He attempted to flick it off without

Raman seeing what he was doing. Appearances must be preserved.

He wondered whether, when it came to it, the old vehicle would start.

But he need not have done. The moment Raman climbed into the driver's seat in front and touched a switch on the polished wood dashboard, two brilliant white beams of light shot out from the headlamps, seeming to illuminate the flat countryside for miles in front. And then, with one pull at the starter, the engine came to life, a deep tigery purr.

They moved smoothly into the night.

But it was soon clear that they were not going to exceed a speed of more than about fifteen miles an hour. That must be what Sir Asif, on his rare trips away from the house, invariably ordered. No wonder the relic vehicle was in such good condition under its layer of dust and cobwebs.

But even at a stately fifteen miles an hour it would not take them long to reach the town, and between their journey's start and its end there was something he intended to do. To pump Raman.

His one previous attempt at this, on the evening of his arrival, had been a dismal failure. 'Oh, sahib, Sir Asif has said I must say nothing.' And that had been that.

But perhaps now, when it looked as if he was leaving the scene of battle, defeated, perhaps he might be able to get from the fellow some information that would be useful, either from the far remoteness of Bombay – noisy, tough, vulgar, friendly Bombay, how he longed to be back in it – or, if he did fall in with Begum Roshan's unlikely plan, almost as remotely from the concealment of the generator shed in Sir Asif's gardens.

He ought to try it. Even though a voice to one side of his head cried out, 'Forget it all, you have done your best, let it go now.' He ought to try. If Sir Asif Ibrahim could hold inflexibly to what he considered his duty, so could Inspector Ganesh Ghote.

He leant forward on the well-sprung broad leather seat

and slid open the glass partition that separated him from the Orderly.

'Raman, do you know that your master is being threatened with death?' he asked bluntly, in the basic Urdu which the Judge customarily used with the Orderly.

'Oh, sahib, many, many times they have threatened. And Judge sahib is always despising.'

'Yes, Raman, but that was in past days, was it not? Did you know that he is threatened still? Threatened today?'

'Judge sahib would not pay heed.'

He leant back to consider a little. In front of him, the Orderly, shoulders flat, back straight, pushed the magnificent old car along at the same steady speed. Its strong headlights beamed out unflickeringly into the velvet, empty night.

Was Raman admitting, from the very obstinacy of his denials, that he did in fact know the contents of the mysterious notes which his master had been receiving? Because certainly the fellow must know that the Judge had had the notes. That much would never escape a servant's eye, accustomed to look as the very essence of his life work at every physical detail surrounding his master. But would he know not simply that the notes had been there, but what had been said in them, what had been typed in them?

Not unless the Judge had told him. He would, of course, have tried to read them when his master was not looking, if he had had the chance, but though he might manage a word or two of English, 'Danger', 'Keep Out', 'No Parking' and the like, it was extremely doubtful whether any fellow of his sort would be able to understand that formal language in which the notes had been written. But might the Judge have told him what had been said in them? No. Or not unless he had wanted from him some information to confirm perhaps a suspicion about who the writer was, that secret tap-tap-tapper on the hidden typewriter. Otherwise a man like Sir Asif would never confide in a servant, however trusted, however long-serving.

Yet could Raman have guessed from his master's attitude that he was worried – for all the old man's calm when he had read that last note, the succession of threats could not have left him totally unmoved – and have realized that the cause must be these mysterious notes? And then have done a little detective work on his own?

Servants like Raman might not be particularly literate, but that did not mean they were not often sharply intelligent.

He decided that the only way he could get round to the far side of the wall of obstinate obedience to Sir Asif's orders which the Orderly had patently erected between the two of them was to adopt a roundabout approach.

He leant a few inches forward again and tried to infuse his voice with casual friendliness.

'You have been a long, long time in Sir Asif's service, isn't it?'

'Yes, sahib.'

Then silence.

Did that wall stretch even further than he had allowed for? Did it encircle the fellow completely?

'Thirty years, sahib. And more now.'

Ah, thank goodness. He was talking. Chatting. Keep it going.

'Thirty years? That is a long time. A really long time. Where was it that you came to him then? Down in the South?'

'Oh yes, sahib. Down far away in the South. Where I was born.'

But silence after that. The flow seemed to have trickled to nothingness again. And the big old car was smoothly eating into the night, the long white beams of its headlamps reaching out. He wished that he knew enough Tamil to speak to the fellow properly in his own language. He was willing to bet he would be talkative all right then. That frequent smile of his surely indicated a basically sunny temperament. A happy chatterer. But conversation in fluent Tamil was beyond the bounds of possibility.

He tried a little more rough-and-ready Urdu. 'Were you a servant in somebody else's house before you became Judge sahib's Orderly?'

'Oh no, sahib. I was not.'

Another silence. They were on a made-up road now, well past the village. The great car's tyres swished steadily on the layer of dust on the tarmac. Time was slipping away fast.

'No, sahib, I was not a servant before. I was in prison.'

'Prison?'

It was the last thing, working his way gently towards his objective, that he had expected to encounter.

'I was an under-trial, sahib. I had been there many months.'

'It happens,' he replied.

It happened still today, he reflected. Indeed, was perhaps worse than in the British days, this waiting and waiting for your trial to begin, coming up before a magistrate for remand time and again.

But what had Raman, feather-light, horseshoe-smiling Raman, done to get himself in gaol?

'But why was it that you were in prison then?'

'Oh, sahib, I had killed.'

'Killed? Killed who?'

He could hardly believe his ears. He knew well enough with the rational side of his mind that all sorts of apparently innocent, easy-going, good-tempered, honest, weak-willed or subservient people could turn out to be murderers. But it had never for one moment remotely struck him that in grinning, attentive, busy Raman the Judge's house was sheltering a killer.

And if he was a killer, why was he in the house at all? How could he possibly have been in the Judge's service for so long? It might be possible that his crime had not been such that it had earned him the death penalty, but it surely must have brought him a long term in gaol. So how, as a man of fifty at most, had he contrived to commit his killing and be free and out of prison more than thirty years ago?

'Sahib, I was killing my cousin.'

'Your cousin?'

'Yes, sahib. My cousin, younger than me by one year, who was always very-very jealous of me, as his father had been always of mine in our village. And one day, when I was eighteen years old, sahib, he attacked me. With a knife, sahib. But I took that knife from him, and then I killed him.'

He thought about the circumstances. On the face of things, Raman should not have been freed after a killing like that. It was not premeditated murder, but it sounded very much as if it had been a good deal more deliberate than a simple accident in the course of a struggle.

'You killed your cousin, and then you were arrested and kept as an under-trial? What was the charge against you?'

'Oh, it was murder, sahib. It was murder.'

'But . . . but you did not serve a long term in gaol?'

'Oh no, sahib. Judge sahib let me go.'

If anything, he felt yet more perplexed. The Judge, Sir Asif, responsible for freeing this man who by his own confession had killed his cousin? Sir Asif freeing him from a murder charge? The Judge who all his life had been haunted by his own leniency in setting free the old Vaishnavite who had then slaughtered his own possibly erring daughter? It did not add up. It simply did not add up.

'Raman, do you know how it came about that the Judge, that Sir Asif, freed you? Do you know that?'

'Oh, sahib, he is saying that it is because of the bus. I am not at all understanding what bus it was, but that is what he is saying. In English, sahib. "False in omnibus," he was saying to me. But that was not truly why he let me go, sahib. It was because I was to be his Orderly. When he was hearing that I did not dare go back to my village, sahib, he said, "You ought to have served thirty years. But I am in need of an Orderly. Do you think you could do those duties?"

And I am answering, "Judge sahib, I will serve you all the time." '

Ghote wanted to laugh.

He also, slightly, wanted to cry.

He thought he could see it all, the actual situation and the wild misconception that had stayed in Raman's head year after year after year. *Falsus in uno, falsus in omnibus.* The Judge himself had quoted the Latin legal principle in telling him about the case of the Vaishnavite singer of holy songs. And, no doubt, it had been on that principle that the Judge had relied in freeing Raman. That case, too, had been a village affair and obviously someone must have tried to improve the evidence against Raman, though in all probability a good deal more gravely than in the Vaishnavite's case. And the Judge, in those distant days, had ruled, very properly, if rigorously, that because the prosecution had put forward some evidence that was clearly not true, the whole of their case must be thrown out. And Raman, poor Raman, his head full of the half-grasped English word 'omnibus', often used then for what everybody nowadays called 'a bus', had believed that Sir Asif, most just of Judges, had seized on something incomprehensible to do with a bus as an excuse to let him off a deserved sentence of thirty years just so that he could become his Orderly.

He wanted to laugh, and to cry.

But – the twin white beams of light were still relentlessly eating into the darkness – there was no time for either laughter or tears. Only for seizing advantage of the mood of easy talkativeness he had induced in Raman to extract from him as many facts as he could about the people in the big house, now minute by minute further away, the people moving daily through its heavy calm, the typewriter users.

Where to begin? Ah, yes.

'So for thirty years and more now you have been serving Sir Asif, is it? And have you served his son also during that time? Have you served Sikander sahib?'

That should do it. That should slide underneath that wall of his. Just let him see that you knew everything, and he would assume that you did.

'No, sahib, no. I have not served Sikander sahib all the time.'

Ha, it had worked. Not a breath of hesitation in the answer.

'No, first I was serving Judge sahib only. Then when he made Begum Roshan stay in the house I was serving her also. But at that time there was an old ayah, an old old woman by the name of Gangubai, who used always to take Sikander sahib his food. Only when she was at last dying did Judge sahib tell me to do it.'

'And did you like doing it? Was Sikander sahib always as mad as he is now?'

'Oh, sahib, that comes and goes. Sometimes he is very quiet for many days. When he is *memboralizing*, sahib.'

'Mem what?'

'*Memboralizing*, sahib. It is meaning telling Government important matters. Sikander Sahib is sometimes *memboralizing* the King Emperor even.'

Memorializing the King Emperor. Of course. Poor mad Sikander was living in the days of the British Raj still. And putting the grievances of his subjugated country to the highest authority.

But the ball must not drop. Keep the easy chat going. There must be more to learn. If there was still time.

'And when he has these quiet days, Sikander Sahib, is he let out from the fort?'

'Oh no, sahib. Never. Never in all the time I have been in the house has he been let out. It would not be safe, sahib. And I was here, you know, even before Judge sahib retired. *May Vacation October Vacation*.'

Again Raman had ventured into English.

He felt proud of himself for having disentangled the slurred syllables. But no time for self-congratulation.

'And Anand Baba, Raman, how long is it since he has been coming to the house?'

'Oh, sahib, for many years. He was once very-very great friend to Sikander Sahib. Two burra Nationalist wallahs together, sahib. And when Sikander Sahib became mad, then Anand Baba, only he was not called that in those days, would come sometimes to see how he was. And later, too, when he had put on his saffron clothes, he came then often.'

'I see. And he has been here long this time?'

'Oh yes, sahib. In the hot weather now Anand Baba does not walk as much as once. He is getting old, sahib. So this time he has stayed and stayed.'

'As long as Judge sahib has been getting the notes?'

But it was a mistake. He knew it as soon as the words were out of his mouth. He had penetrated the outer wall of Raman's defences but there was an inner wall there as well, and one not to be slid under by guile.

The flat shoulders on the other side of the glass panel hunched a little, and for the first time the big car gained noticeably in speed.

Then silent minutes later they were pulling up outside the railway station in the town. He took his sad tan suitcase from Raman and handed him a small sum, seeing suddenly in his mind's eye the soft browny-white paper of an expenses application resting on the familiar surface of his desk in his cabin back at Headquarters.

'If there is no train,' he said, 'I will be able to spend the night in the station retiring room.'

'Oh yes, sahib. Good night, sahib. Thank you, sahib.'

The big car purred away, white headlamp beams swirling round in a wide circle.

But he would not be entering the station, routing out the stationmaster, inspecting the accommodation offered by the retiring room, perhaps insisting that a sweeper be wakened to improve it and eventually spending a quiet night there. If he entered the station at all it would simply be for the purpose of sending some telegrams to Headquarters in

Bombay inquiring what was known about Father Adam and Mr Dhebar. Because he no longer had any intention of waiting for a train. He had learnt too much during that long fifteen-mile-an-hour car journey for there to be any question now of abandoning his assignment.

CHAPTER XI

WALKING THROUGH the dark streets of the town, past the huddle of upturned tongas near the station with the odour of their horses tethered nearby rich on the night air, past the Variety Hall cinema, past two small temples, round the corner at the Mission College, Ghote felt his renewed sense of purpose strong upon him. All right, he had not learnt anything wonderfully startling from Raman as Sir Asif's big old car had swished along on its journey, but he had discovered a few hard facts to get his teeth into. Gone at last was that sheer floating helplessness he had been so conscious of, lying all the long stiflingly hot afternoon on that high hard bed under the ridiculous grunting old inefficient fan. Errr-bock. Errr-bock.

Now he had some solid pieces of information to think about. The Saint, for one. If you looked at the case from a strictly factual viewpoint – and that was the way things should be looked at, damn it – the Saint was now a firm suspect. He had had, it was now clear, the opportunity to deliver the threatening notes: he had been a visitor to the house during the whole period they had been received. And he had had the means to produce them too: he was an educated man, and if there was a typewriter somewhere in that house, and there must be, then he could have banged out the notes on it. And, it was now clear too, he had a possible motive: had he not been a Nationalist fighter in the old days, a friend and probably mentor of the rabid Sikander Ibrahim? Quite conceivably then, for reasons certainly not precisely plain still, he had waited until now to exact revenge, a slow revenge, on the man who had pronounced the death sentences in the Madurai Conspiracy Case of long ago.

A second item, more negative but still decent hard information: it was clear beyond doubt now that Sikander Ibrahim could not be the person he was looking for. He had never been let out of that prison down underneath the ruins of the fort. It had always been, quite plainly, too unsafe to risk anything of the sort. The man was a volcanic force, liable to erupt at any instant, however long he had been quietly *memboralizing* the King Emperor, liable without warning to spew destruction over every barrier. And that, odd though it was, put him right out of account as a possible murderer.

But he had learnt another positive hard fact. Begum Roshan, she had been made to come and live in the isolated old house. 'He made Begum Roshan stay in the house,' those had been Raman's very words. And there she had remained, never marrying, watching the years pass. So here was somebody with a real grievance against Sir Asif. Agreed it was not clear why she should have waited so long before suddenly acting against him, or even just what it was she might hope to gain by sending him the threatening notes, but here still was a hard fact to take into account. And it was splendidly reassuring to have at last some hard facts in the matter.

Something to get one's teeth into at last.

Keeping in his head Begum Roshan's plan of the town, which he had carefully studied under the light of the sole municipal lamp-standard he had encountered, he turned off into the narrow street in which the offices of *The Sputnik* (Weekly Publication Assured) were situated. And there at the far end there was a light shining from an upper window.

He imagined Mr Dhebar sitting up there composing far into the night the latest in the long series of editorials with which he proposed, aided a little by the stringent comments of the man who had pronounced the Madurai sentences, to wake up India.

He picked his way rapidly as he could down the narrow street, just able in the darkness to make out and avoid the shallow central drain running all along it.

And, sure enough, when he reached the place where the light from the upper storey window was pouring dimly on to the narrow sleeping street, he was able to make out a handsome white signboard on which was painted, in a dignified and flowing style, 'The Sputnik', with below, in smaller but no less dignified letters, its editor's name together with the fact that he held the BA degree of Ahmedabad University.

He knocked on the narrow door beside this notice. He waited. Nothing seemed to happen inside. He knocked again. And still the house stayed as silent as if it was deserted. The light from the window over his head nevertheless continued to shine steadily, if dimly, out. He knocked a third time, long and loud. Nearby a dog began to bark.

But now there was a change at the window above. A shifting of shadows and at last a pale face at the bars.

'Mr Dhebar?' he called up. 'It is I. Insp – It is Doctor Ghote. We met at Sir Asif Ibrahim's.'

'One moment. I will come.'

A long pause. The sound of chappals flap-flapping down wooden stairs. Then, not the rattle of a chain being unhooked from behind the door, but, surely, the more cautious clink of one being hooked up. And a moment later the door opened, just three inches and no more.

The pear-heavy face of Mr Dhebar peered out, solidly determined not to let any unscrutinized individual penetrate his threshold, perhaps to seize the secret files long accumulated by The Sputnik.

'Begum Roshan told me to come to you,' he said, already feeling that it was altogether unlikely that the editor would be willing to do all that Sir Asif's daughter asked.

But her name certainly seemed to be a password.

'Begum Roshan sent?' Mr Dhebar's lugubrious face lit up. 'But come in, my dear chap, come in. If you are here on behalf of Begum Roshan you are thrice welcome.'

The chain was hastily removed, the door swept open. He stepped inside. Vaguely by the light coming down the sharp open flight of stairs in front of him he could make out that there was only one room on the ground floor, an office with a counter running across it and a large clock with roman numerals hanging on the far wall, its hands proclaiming the unlikely hour of five o'clock. Propped up against the counter was Mr Dhebar's motor-scooter.

Prompted by the sight of it, he explained concisely as he could what he wanted from his host, though he avoided giving any reason why it was necessary for him to be going through such curious manoeuvres. Even as he produced his proposition he could not help thinking that it surely far exceeded the bounds of any polite request. It was damned cheek, in fact.

But Mr Dhebar agreed to it without a moment's hesitation. 'Yes, yes. By all means. You should leave about one hour before dawn. The machine is not immensely speedy, though reliable, reliable, I am glad to say. And I have an alarm clock, so I will see to it that you get off in good time. Yes, yes, if Begum Roshan wants this, I will do all in my power to see to it. Yes.'

But then there came a sudden glance of doubt, a shrewdness. 'Unless you are returning for the purposes of an assignation with the lady. That would be going too far.'

He looked back at him in the dim light, wooden-faced.

'Excuse my joke,' Mr Dhebar said hastily. 'Excuse my joke, in rather poor taste, I fear.'

He felt yet more ill at ease. The editor's suggestion had not sounded like a joke. He tried, not very successfully, to bring a smile up on to his lips.

'Well, well,' Mr Dhebar said with forced briskness, 'come up to my humble chamber, my dear chap. Not palatial. Not palatial at all. But such as it is you are welcome to it.

And you should get to bed right away. The morrow will be upon us with stealthy foot all too soon. Yes, all too soon.'

He followed the editor's tightly bulky figure up the steep stairs and into the single room which appeared to form the whole of the top part of the little house. Evidently, from the drooping-cord charpoy in one corner, it was where Mr Dhebar spent his bachelor nights. But the bed was put into complete insignificance by mounds and heaps everywhere of newspapers and magazines, fresh at the top, yellowed and ancient at the bottom. There was the *Times of India*, going back, it seemed, almost to British days. There were piles of the *Statesman* from Calcutta and the *Hindu* from Madras, both every bit as aged. There were the coloured covers of the *Illustrated Weekly*, dozens and dozens and dozens of them. There was Bombay's *Blitz*, gaudy red headlines long faded to an undemanding pink.

Beyond these, the room was almost unfurnished. Except that under the single uncovered light bulb there was a little rickety table with on it a typewriter.

A typewriter. He looked at it with all the passion of a small boy contemplating a piled tray of sweetmeats at a meethaiwallah's stall. He longed simply to advance upon it, slip in a sheet of paper, type with all the rapidity that two battering fingers were capable of THEQUICKBROWNFOX JUMPEDOVERTHELAZYDOG, and then hide that useful piece of evidence somewhere on his person ready for comparison with the next note that Sir Asif Ibrahim might receive, however difficult that would be to get hold of.

But with Mr Dhebar solemnly regarding him there was nothing to be done.

Perhaps if the fellow went out for a moment . . . But he did not.

'Kindly avail yourself of my humble resting place,' he said instead. 'I shall continue to work if the light does not disturb you. Consulting my files. My amassed files.'

He laid a benedictory hand on the top of the tallest *Times of India* pile and then sat himself down cross-legged on the floor beside it, evidently ready to extract from its layers whatever piece of the long-recorded past particularly interested him at this moment.

Stretching himself cautiously on the slack-corded charpoy on the other side of the room, he discovered that it needed the attentions of the carpenter yet more urgently than he had thought. It did not just sag, it sagged unevenly. Its only taut rope bit into his hip like an instrument of torture.

'Yes,' Mr Dhebar continued plummily, 'these files, I am accustomed to say, are my true friends. My only counsellors. It is from them that I learn all that has happened in the past of our wretched country from its first day as a nation. It is from their wise aid that I draw every lesson necessary for the future. The light does not worry you?'

For a fleeting second Ghote was tempted to answer the added question as if it was not a small practical inquiry but a large moral one. And to answer deflatingly. But he owed the editor some politeness.

'No, no. Please keep it on. I would not like to prevent you from continuing your valuable work.'

'Well, yes, it is true that it is here, toiling often like this deep into the night, that I make my little discoveries. Sometimes even my not so little discoveries.'

No, this was carrying self-esteem too far. He closed his eyes.

'It was here, for instance,' the remorseless plummy voice continued, 'that I hit upon the facts that made me aware, poignantly aware, shall I say, of our friend Begum Roshan's sad situation.'

He opened his eyes.

Was that squat figure sitting dumpily there on the floor beside his pile of old newspapers, his head level with his own on the charpoy, going to add to that remark? Or was it intended to stand on its own as some sort of test? A way of finding out if he too was aware of the sad situation? Was in Begum Roshan's confidence?

To prompt the fellow? Or to leave a silence?

He left a silence. And eventually Mr Dhebar gave a heavy sigh.

'Yes, there it all was in my filed copies of *The Hindu*. There for any person able to read between the lines.'

Another long melancholy sign.

Now he would have to be prompted. Now he wanted to be.

'And you were able to read between those lines, Mr Dhebar?'

'Ah, yes. Yes, I was. The poor woman. The poor, poor woman. First, the announcement of her forthcoming marriage. And the name of the bridegroom-elect not a Muslim one. All too easy to imagine, in those days some thirty years ago, what had gone on behind the scenes before that announcement was printed. What was still going on when it was printed.'

'Yes,' he answered, attempting to infuse an equal weightiness into the word.

To get hold of the rest of this he would cross and cross again the line that divided proper interest from gross flattery.

He shifted a little on the wretched charpoy and managed to transfer the cutting pressure to a different part of his hip.

And, besides, what the fellow had said was true enough. Thirty years ago divisions between the religious communities were very much sharper than they were today, and they were not so easily crossed even now. So before a Muslim girl's marriage to someone outside her community would have been publicly announced, there would indeed have been trouble behind the scenes.

'Yes,' he repeated, with a sigh in his turn. 'And you said first an announcement of a forthcoming marriage. But Begum Roshan has never married. So there was another announcement?'

'Yes, yes. There was. The marriage arranged between Mr So-and-So – I have forgotten the name now, but I can always find it again in my files if you wish . . .'

'No, no. Kindly do not trouble yourself.'

'No? Well, he was a young lawyer from a well-known South Indian family, married long since to another lady, from his own community, of course. And dead now also. But there it was, the second announcement: "The marriage will not now take place." '

'And it would have been soon after that that Begum Roshan came to live here, in this remote locality?'

'Yes. Yes, soon after. I have understood that from her. There is, you know, a certain sympathy between us. An unexpressed sympathy.'

'Yes.'

Unexpressed that sympathy was, he reflected. Begum Roshan had not seemed to have much time for the visiting editor.

But he had learnt from the fellow something worth knowing. Another piece of hard fact. Something else requiring adjustments to his picture of life in the old quiet house.

Firmly he shut his eyes again. But Mr Dhebar apparently failed to notice.

'Yes,' came that voice, musing in tone but with a heavy undernote of beetle-buzzing determination. 'Yes, things today are not as they were. Today there would not be such objection to a marriage across the religious line. Not at all, not at all.'

But he ignored the solemn reflections.

Not so long before, as he had been making his way through the town's dark streets, he had wondered to himself why on earth Begum Roshan should have waited till now to leave death threats for her father. And here, unexpectedly, he had been given an answer. Thirty years ago it would have been, beyond doubt, Sir Asif who had been in the end responsible for preventing her marriage. And that would have been at much the same time as he had been pronouncing those death sentences on the Madurai Conspirators. Another death then, perhaps, added to them. A death of the heart. Yes, it made a sort of sense for Begum Roshan to choose to link the Madurai case to her own long-nurtured revenge.

If she had. Because there was no proof of any of it. No proof at all. The evidence he had, such as it was, told just as much against the Saint or against that awful white Naxalite. Or, come to that, against Mr Dhebar here.

The figures and the faces loomed up one by one and in curious combinations in his mind's eye. The Saint, sitting cross-legged, smiling his sledge-hammer smile from among the falling white locks of his gushing beard. Mr Dhebar, approaching the old house on his motor-scooter through the still heat of the sun-battered afternoon like a little buzzing insect determined to bore its way through any obstacle, Begum Roshan, twisting and twisting at the edge of her sari, taking up defensive position after defensive position and abandoning one after the other, last stand after last stand. The American priest with his tangled eyebrows and necktie loosely knotted below the collar of his checked shirt, talking interminably about 'conventional morality', 'the capitalist media', 'armed struggle' and 'the oppressor class'. The Saint and the American. The American and Mr Dhebar. Mr Dhebar and Begum Roshan. Begum Roshan and Mr Dhebar.

And, though he had been sure he would not sleep on his abominably uncomfortable charpoy, with the light still burning and Mr Dhebar cross-legged beside his high-piled file of the *Times of India* palpably present, those whirling and conjoined figures suddenly brought sleep to him.

The strident ringing of Mr Dhebar's large old alarm-clock woke him as suddenly.

He opened his eyes wide. The editor was standing over him, a sombre expression on his large pear face.

'What – What is it?' he asked him, prey to inexplicable fears.

'It is time for you to set forth,' Mr Dhebar replied. 'Time to set forth if you are to get back to the house as early as you wish.'

'Oh yes,' he answered, rationality reasserting its precarious hold. 'Yes. Thank you.'

He heaved himself off the charpoy. His left hip felt
cripplingly stiff where the taut cord had cut and cut into it.
Following the editor sleepily, he went down the steep
flight of stairs and out to the bathroom at the back. By the
time he had finished, Mr Dhebar had taken his tan suitcase,
strapped it on to the back of the scooter and wheeled the
machine out into the street.

He went out into the cool pre-dawn dark and joined him.

'Turn right at the top, my dear fellow, and then keep
straight on. Straight on, straight on, till you see the house
on the far side of the river.'

He muttered a few words of thanks, took the handlebars
of the scooter and pushed it up the length of the narrow
street, unwilling to wake Mr Dhebar's neighbours by
starting up the noisy little engine. Then, at the top, he put a
leg over the bouncy black saddle, switched on the headlight
and kicked the machine into life.

And he was off, buzzing through the darkness, heading
once again for that big old time-smothered house and the
long tin shed in its gardens from which he was to attempt to
save Sir Asif Ibrahim from his own obstinacy.

But he refused to let thoughts of the difficulty of his task
depress him. The air was delicious on his face and body,
puffing out his shirt behind him, sending his necktie put
on in honour of Sir Asif's 'Drinks Before Dinner' the night
before flicking like a whip, making him cool as he had not
felt ever since he had first arrived. The road was clear in
front, a straight ribbon, and he was making progress. He
must be.

The eastern sky had just begun to lighten by the smallest
amount when he whirred past the village and came to the
river. He cut off the machine's engine and pushed it rapidly
as he could across the stony river bed, half afraid that some
servant in the big house on the far side, Raman perhaps,
might be up and about this early and would see him from an
upper window or that the watchman had for once broken
with the routine Begum Roshan had told him about and had

stayed in the gardens till now.

But all seemed silent and still. Almost an hour before the milkman, with his swinging-uddered cow and its muzzled calf, would make his appearance.

He mounted the far slope of the river and made his way, steadily as he could, through the gardens to the long tin shed under the old tamarind tree. Heaving the scooter back on to its stand, he tried the shed door. No padlock, thank goodness. But the broad corrugated iron door shuddered appallingly as he began to pull it wide. He stopped, took a new hold, lifted it half an inch from the ground and tried again.

And managed it in silence.

He wheeled the scooter into the thick, oil-smelling darkness and found, to his delight, that there was room to push it right to the far end, past the bulky shape of the generator engine, past a great block of aged batteries and round behind the long fuel tank itself, made out more by feel than sight at this dark end of the long shed. But with luck it should be safe here. There ought to be no need for Raman, when he came in the evening to start the ancient chugging engine, to penetrate as far as this. Very probably he would be able to stay here himself while the Orderly, that murderer long ago, carried out his task.

He went back and carefully closed the door and then, stopping only to slip a pair of comfortable chappals out of his case and put into it cramping shoes and socks, he settled down on the beaten earth floor close by the hidden machine.

When it was day he might perhaps by peering through some nail hole in the corrugated iron sheets of the shed be able to catch a glimpse of one of the inhabitants of the now sleeping house walking in the gardens before it grew too hot. Perhaps from them he could get some idea of what was going on, hear a snatch of talk possibly, or see Begum Roshan and be able to attract her attention. Otherwise it was a matter of patiently waiting.

Half-dozing, he was aware vaguely of the swiftly in-

creasing daylight outside. Then at last he heard the frantic
hoarse bleating of the milkman's muzzled calf and a little
later the sound of women from the village singing down
by the river where they had begun to wash clothes.

Then, quite suddenly, loud against the background of
that distant sound, he heard Raman coming towards him.
The fellow was singing as well, light-heartedly and even
loudly singing the same South Indian boatman's song he had
heard him humming the evening before as he had passed by
in the dark coming back from taking Sikander his evening
food.

He crouched up in abrupt tension. What if Begum Roshan
was wrong about the fellow's routine? What if every morning
he looked into the shed to see if the generator was all right?
What if he even carried out a thorough inspection of the
whole oily-smelling building?

It was not beyond the bounds of possibility.

He imagined the Orderly coming along the winding path
from the house. He would be carrying held out in front of
him the same large tray he had taken through the moonlit
darkness. Under its draped white cloth on banana-leaf
plates now would be whatever food the violent Sikander was
given in the mornings. Fewer leaves, probably, than the
three of last night. And Raman would be wearing his neat
white jacket, meeting the standard Sir Asif had set more
than thirty years before when he had taken on the fellow.
'False in omnibus', and believing it all this time. What a
changeless world they both lived in.

But would that world change suddenly and totally in just
eleven days from now?

The sound of the boat song was getting louder and louder
in the morning air. The fellow must be happy. Was he
always happy at the start of each day? Happy until he
encountered the first of Sir Asif's rages, and then happy
again within minutes of that blasting? Evidently the fellow
did not regard having to look after the madman underneath
the old fort as a burden. Perhaps on most mornings he was

able to greet him cheerfully, have some friendly chat. Perhaps it was only on rare days that he would be confronted by the raging maniac he himself had seen down in the darkness there.

And now the sound of Raman's singing was only yards away. Was it going to pass the shed door?

In the gloom, pierced, now that the sun had risen, by a good many thin beams of bright light coming through nail holes and slits in the walls, he began to count in his head. If he could get up to twenty that was bound to mean the Orderly was safely past.

One, two, three . . .

He must be right outside.

Keep counting, keep counting.

. . . eight, nine, ten, eleven.

Was the sound fading? Just a little? Impossible to tell. Count.

. . . seventeen, eighteen, nineteen, twenty.

Yes. Twenty. And he had gone past. No doubt about it. And stupid to have got into a panic like that. Yes, possible in theory that he would have come in and made his way right to the back here. But not really something that was likely to happen.

He must make himself be sensible. Within the bounds of possibility, what rot.

He straightened his legs on the hard earth floor.

How long would Raman be today down in the bat-smelling darkness under the fort? In what state would he find the captive? Raging and shaking at the bars? Or talking about 'memboralizing' the King Emperor?

The sounds of day outside went lazily on. The village women's voices in the distance, birds twittering, the tiny noises of innumerable insects.

Then suddenly, totally unexpected in the tranquillity, there came a wild screaming bellow. A wild screaming human bellow.

He jumped to his feet.

Sikander.

It sounded for all the world like Sikander, like the howl of
rage that had greeted him down in the dark under the fort.
But how could it seem to come from so near? From outside?

Then, thumping hard on the sun-baked earth, came the
noise of running feet. And a low moaning, the moan of
someone running in fear.

Raman. It must be Raman.

A moment later, horribly loud in the air now, there was
another wild bellow. There could be no doubt any longer.
Sikander had escaped, was out in the garden, was in pursuit
of Raman.

What to do?

Only one thing possible.

He dodged through the gloom, past the fuel tank, past
the bank of batteries, past the generator and its motor and
wrenched open the awkward door of the shed. At once he
saw, in the bright dazzle of the morning light, what the
situation was. Raman was pelting towards the house, hair
streaming back in the wind of his speed. And bounding
after him at a yet greater pace was the boulder-chested,
wildly bearded form of Sikander. Arms outstretched. Huge
hands already clutching for a throat.

Without pause for thought, he set out after him.

But – he knew it even as he started – he was going to be too
late. He was still fifteen or twenty yards distant when
Sikander caught up with the Orderly. With a yet louder
yell of triumphant fury he seized him by the neck and
actually plucked him up off the ground. He raised the slim,
threshing body high above him and then crashed forward
with it on to the hard ground with a thick thump of sound.

He leapt forward in a long dive, felt himself jar against
the wild man's back as if he had flung himself on to a rock,
found he had managed to dig both forearms in across his
tree-thick neck and, thrusting his knees into the ground on
either side, began to heave upwards with all the force he
could put into back and legs.

For what seemed an impossibly long time, for what must have been a full minute, he thought he was not going to budge the mad giant by an inch. Sikander had his teeth fastened into the flesh of Raman's shoulder. Deep into his prey.

But then at last he felt that boulder-chested body coming slowly up. And then there was a convulsive stiffening in the muscles hard up against his own. In a moment the wild creature would fling himself round. Those huge hands would be reaching for his own throat.

Only one thing to do. He loosed his right arm, raised it, turned it so that his hand was flat and hard and brought it chopping down.

Below him Sikander slumped suddenly back, all relaxation.

CHAPTER XII

RAMAN WAS IN a pretty poor way. Sikander Ibrahim's unbridled violence had almost squeezed the life out of him and there were, too, deep bite wounds in the fleshy lower part of his neck. That much Ghote had seen as soon as he had staggered to his feet and taken a quick look at the prostrate Orderly.

He went back then to Sikander, happily still unconscious, hastily stripped the tie from round his own neck and used it to fasten the madman's wrists before dragging him foot by foot over to the nearest bush and getting the other end of the tie secured to its base. It was not very safe, but he hoped it would hold at least until he had broken the news up at the house.

By the time he had completed the task, pushing and heaving at the heavy barrel-like body, Raman was half sitting up on the wiry brown grass where he had been felled. He walked back over to him.

'How are you?' he asked. 'Do you think you can get up to the house if I give you a shoulder to rest on?'

Raman groaned.

But he did begin to make an effort to get to his feet, and soon, with a little assistance, he was standing upright. Together they made a slow journey to the house, standing tall and powdery in the first bright fresh rays of the soon-to-be-conquering sun.

He took him in at the main door, regardless of any proprieties, and lowered him on to one of the marble benches in the wide hallway. The sound of their arrival brought a maidservant to peer at them for a moment like a scared deer round the corner, and a minute or two later Begum Roshan arrived, tautly ready for crisis.

His attempt to forestall this by rapidly telling her what had happened and asking her to find the mali from the gardens, the cook and any other menservants to get Sikander back into his prison failed completely.

'I knew it, I knew it,' she exclaimed, ignoring his urgent practical plea. 'I knew that one day this would happen. I warned and I warned. But he would not listen. He would not allow an Ibrahim to be put into a common madhouse. I said that one day he would break out, and now he has. Now he has.'

'Yes,' he said, soothingly as he could. 'But, madam, please would you find people to get him back. I was not able to tie him very well. He would break loose when he becomes conscious again.'

But again Begum Roshan seemed not to have heard. She went over to Raman, lying back limply on the bench, and took him by the shoulders, her bone-thin fingers digging hard into his dirtied and crumpled white jacket.

'What did you do?' she demanded. 'How did you let him out? Why did this happen? I knew it would. I said it would. But no one would pay any attention. No attention at all.'

Raman had given a little gasp of pain when she had seized him, but he managed to offer a reply.

'Oh, memsahib, memsahib, sometimes I have to unlock the gate there. To fetch out food he has left. But, memsahib, I do not do it if it is one of the bad days. But today I thought he was sleeping.'

'You fool,' Begum Roshan shouted. 'You should never unlock that gate. Never, never, never. Once you do it, then it is too late. Too late altogether, you fool.'

Raman bowed his head under her onslaught, the grey hair at its centre where the dye had grown out suddenly visible. It was almost as if he was preparing to receive a physical beating

But then a quiet voice spoke behind them.

'Raman, you have been hurt?'

It was Sir Asif. Once again, hearing a disturbance, he must have walked holding his black cane up in the air so as to come upon the scene unawares.

Now the old Judge made his way quickly across to the Orderly and looked down at him. There was real concern on that nose-flattened, impervious face.

'Sir, I could not help,' Raman said. 'Sikander sahib was pretending to be asleep still. Sir, I . . . I tried . . .'

'Yes, yes. But what did he do to you? He is not a reasoning man, you know, when he is bad. He is a creature without checks.'

'He was going to choke me, sahib. And – and he bit my neck, sahib, like a tiger.'

'Let me look.'

The old man put his fleshless, high-veined hands gently on to the Orderly's jacket and peeled it back a little from the shoulder. The half-dozen deep little wounds had almost ceased to bleed, but they still looked very much like the bite, not of a tiger, but certainly of some vicious animal.

The Judge sighed.

'Go with Begum Roshan,' he said to Raman. 'She will find something to put on there.' He straightened up. 'And Sikander?' he asked. 'Has anyone gone to look for him?'

'Sir,' Raman said, 'Doctor Ghote tied him to a tree.'

Then Sir Asif saw him. His face hardened in an instant. 'What – what are you doing here?' he said.

'Sir,' Raman interrupted, 'he jumped on Sikander sahib and he pulled him away from me.'

Sir Asif gave him a long steady look.

'Well then, Doctor Ghote,' he said at last, 'I shall have the pleasure of seeing you at luncheon, I hope. But just now, if you will excuse me, I must make sure my son is taken to a place of safety.'

'Yes, Sir Asif,' he answered.

He felt abruptly swept through by a dragging weight of tiredness. It came with the recognition, fought off till this moment, that had he been just a little unlucky in getting in his knock-out blow to Sikander, almost certainly the creature without checks, as Sir Asif had called him, would have savaged him as well as Raman to death.

He headed for the stairs and, above, his own room, or what had been his room. It would hardly have been occupied by any new guest, he thought.

He felt an overwhelming need to retreat, to curl up, to hide for a while.

The room was just as he had left it. Sunlight was already streaming in through the unclosed shutters, dazzling and beginning to be unpleasantly hot if not yet mercilessly beating down all beneath it. He flicked at the brown bakelite switch for the fan. It gave the soft hollow click he remembered from before, and the ancient apparatus hanging at its slight angle from the ceiling lurched into slow movement. He dragged himself across to the window and heaved the shutters closed, returned almost staggering now and allowed himself to fall full-length across the high hard bed.

Errr-bock. Errr-bock. The fan above him ground out its message. The house is still here, it said. Nothing has changed. Nothing, if the house has its way, will ever change. Errr-bock. Errr-bock.

But something had changed. He himself was a new factor in the situation. He had been allowed to insert himself into the time-hardened pattern, the Deputy Commissioner's wedge, and he had begun simply by his presence to alter that pattern, to edge it into a new shape. And then he had been rejected, spat out. As, looking back, it was almost certain that sooner or later he would have been. But now he was here once more. Again the wedge was in. And this time, thanks to the chance of having been able to save poor Raman, he would not be so easy to dislodge. Sir Asif's sense of justice, binding the old man like a constricting band growing out of his own skin, would make sure of that.

And, once again inside the boundaries of the old house, he would act. He would jar forwards little by little. Sir Asif would not want it any more than he had done before. But now he would not be able to be stopped. However small the steps he was able to take, they would alter the time-frozen state of affairs. Little by little.

In the bare room the heat, despite the thickness of the old seared-wood shutters, despite the churning of the ancient fan, began to build up. He lay unmoving, just where he had collapsed face foremost on to the wide hard white mattress. For now he felt such a languor in every limb that any action seemed impossible.

But that would not last.

There were things that soon he could do. Things he would do. He would go and find the Saint and talk to him. He would tackle him about the old days, the British days. He would see whether those long-ago inflicted wounds were still festering. And if he got no response? If it was another day of silence? Wait and see. Perhaps it would be best not to try and cross that barrier till it was taken down. As sooner or later it must be. The Saint would not be silent for ever. And nor was that the only route open. There was Begum Roshan, too. He would go soon and talk to her. And suddenly spring on her what he now knew about that marriage that had never been, and watch her then, watch her like a kite hovering above the ever-moving city ready to plummet down the moment some tiny movement below signalled prey. And he would talk to the American again, sound him out about what exactly he felt over the project to blast the bund and change the course of the old river, see if even by a hair's breadth he crossed the far borders of rationality and betrayed himself as a killer. Finally, he would talk once more with the Judge. He had the right now. He would ask him in turn about each of the people in the house and about Mr Dhebar, that regular visitor, and this time he would prise from him the facts he needed to know.

Errr-bock. Errr-bock. Errr-bock.

Damn fan. Damn useless noisy object.

He slept a little. Woke with a start. Slept again. Woke again. Scrabbled up on the hard bed and, screwing up his eyes, inspected his wristwatch.

Almost midday.

The room now was like a closed oven. Outside, he could see through the gaps in the old shutters, the light was vibrating in its intensity. There was no sound other than the seemingly yet slower grunting of the old fan.

That ever-hesitating errr-bock, errr-bock, maddening within minutes.

He slid off the bed and went into the little bathroom. A wash and a mouth rinse in the tepid water from the large brass *lota* did a little, though not much, to refresh him. He straightened his clothes. At some stage he would have to have his suitcase up from its hiding-place at the back of the generator shed. But not now.

Soon downstairs it would be time for lunch. So somewhere there the other members of the household, the typewriter users and Sir Asif were to be found. Time now, then, to push inwards. Perhaps only a little. But as much and as far and as hard as he could.

His mouth felt dry again despite the water he had rinsed it with.

Who first?

Well, let chance give the answer.

He left the airless room, walked slowly along the equally

airless, musty-smelling passage, came to the stairs and went
down them, creating only the slightest cooling movement in
the air by trotting downwards, letting the weight of his
languidly heavy body take him.

As he reached the stairs' foot by the tall newel-post carved
in the half resemblence of a head, he heard swift footsteps
coming along the passage to his left. He turned. It was
Raman.

'Well,' he asked him, 'are you feeling all right again?'

'Oh yes, Doctor sahib. I am very-very well now. But,
sahib, you have saved my life. I kiss your feet.'

He had to catch him by the upper arms to prevent him
actually doing so.

'Look,' he said quickly, 'there is something you can do
for me.'

'Oh yes, Doctor sahib. Anything at all. Anything that is
in my power to do, that I will do.'

'Well, perhaps it is not a great deal. Let me tell you. I have
a favour to ask your master. Something that perhaps he
would not too much like. So I want to know the best time to
ask him. When he is not . . . not too tired.'

Raman looked at him. There was no grin for once on his
thin and eager face.

'Oh, Doctor sahib, I am well understanding. And it is
difficult. Judge sahib is stern always. But – ' he hesitated –
'but now, I think might be the best time of all, sahib. Now,
this moment. He is in the library. He is smoking. The pipe is
going well, well. Now would be the time, sahib. Now.'

He felt a sharp downward lurch in the pit of his stomach.
He had decided to let chance dictate whom in the household
he would see first. But of all of them it was the Judge he
least wanted to tackle. And now chance had thrown him the
Judge in this way.

'Yes,' he said to Raman. 'Yes, it would seem that now is
the best time. Thank you.'

He turned and walked along towards the library.

What resources did he have, he asked himself. What

resources? All very well to think of himself as the Deputy Commissioner's wedge. All very well to talk of pushing and pushing and to say that he could not be rejected now. But he was up against a stone wall, an iron wall.

He felt sweat appear on the sides of his face and underneath his chin.

He scrabbled almost frantically at his mind to find something to use in the encounter ahead.

And found it.

Sikander. He would use Sikander. But not as he had tried to use him before when the Judge had contemptuously rejected his blackmailing. No, that had been quite the wrong way to go about it. It was never the way to tackle a man like Sir Asif. But there was a way in which he could make use of that poor demented creature, now back in his underground prison.

Quite clearly, now that Sikander had once escaped, it was more than ever right that he should be taken to some State institution where he could be properly guarded. But instead, as soon as he saw the Judge, he would offer to keep his secret always, despite what should be his duty. He would make him that offer freely and at once, and then surely in exchange the old man would take him fully into his confidence.

He knocked at the library door.

He heard through the solid teak the Judge's voice calling out and put his hand on the door-knob. His sweat-covered palm slithered round on it uselessly.

But at last he succeeded in turning it and thrust open the door.

The Judge was sitting where he had seen him before, in the fine high-backed chair with at his side the table with the hookah on it. He was holding the mouthpiece in his hand.

The sound of the pipe's throaty bubbling, cool and mellow, came clearly to him.

'Sir Asif,' he said, 'there was something I wished to say to you.'

'Come in, my dear fellow. Take a seat, take a seat. There is something I, too, wish to say to you.'

He pulled another of the high-backed heavy chairs slightly towards the Judge and sat on its edge.

'Sir – '

'No, my dear fellow, let me say my say first. It is this. You, today, have done me an immeasurable service. You know about poor Sikander. He has been that way for years. It was something that began to come upon him in the British days. His rabid patriotism then was no more than a symptom of what was happening to him, little though we realized it at the time. I used to say that he had become an agitator because he was fit for no other profession. A judgement that could certainly be made of more than a few of the other thrusting so-called patriots of that day, to my mind. But not to Sikander. Not to Sikander, as it turned out. No, he was no agitator but a poor boy in a state of agitation, a state of agitation that grew quickly to complete madness. Naturally I sought medical opinions, and from them I learnt that there was nothing to be done. So I decided to confine him out here. I had hoped that he could be confined in safety. I saw no reason why he should not be.'

A gnarled hand clutched at the arm of the chair.

'Until today. Until today I saw no reason why he should not be confined here in complete safety.'

The old man came to a halt.

Sitting opposite, he felt himself poised hovering, poised like a diver above a turbulent sea.

Then 'Sir,' he said, 'I myself still see no reason why that confinement here should not continue to go on.'

He fixed his gaze on the Judge's face. Now it was much easier to see in the tall book-lined room than when he had last confronted the intractable old man. The white blaze of the sun was forcing its way in, even despite the chick blinds.

And bit by bit he saw, plainly written on the dry skin, clear in the sunken eyes on either side of that flattened beak of a nose, a slow look of covetousness grow and spread.

He had offered a gift that the aged Judge and father wanted to his innermost depths to have.

A sharp regret went across his mind like the tip of a knife blade jaggedly tearing. His intransigent opponent was after all going to succumb. That unbending will was softening, melting like ugly wax.

The eyes were lowered now. The chin sunk on the breast.

In the big muffled room it was silent, as silent as if the place had remained unentered ever in all the long hot airless years since it had been built. Even the hookah on the table had ceased to give out the least intermittent bubbling.

He almost burst out, 'No. No, sir, do not say it. Be angry instead. Order me out. Refuse. Reject me.'

Then, with a small lift of the head, the Judge began to speak.

'Inspector, let me tell you a story. The story of an incident that occurred to me many, many years ago when I was an Assistant Collector, a callow youth, just returned to India from Cambridge, thinking that I knew everything and proud as Lucifer of my new appointment, an appointment which took in, of course, a good deal of judicial work on tour.' The eyes were now fully on him. 'I had come one day to a certain village, a place of some size, where I knew that the headman had a considerable interest in a land tenure case due to come before me. So I was not at all surprised to find on my first morning there that I was the recipient of a "dolly", as my British colleagues used to call them.'

'That is a *dali*? A basket of fruit?'

'Yes, yes.'

The old man sounded decidedly petulant at the interruption. It was plain that, having chosen this curious way of succumbing to the offer, perhaps because somehow he saw in it a way of justifying to himself what he was about to do, he was weighing each word of his story as he told it.

'Now you know, of course, that it was perfectly permissible to accept such gifts, provided that they were only of either *phool* or *phal*, flowers or fruit. But, as soon as I lifted from that generous basket two or three little brown chikoos, a fruit of which I was always particularly fond, I saw that on the bottom there had been laid a five-hundred-rupee note.' Again those deep-sunk eyes bore into him. 'Well, Inspector, I was a young man then, as I told you. Can you guess what I did?'

He thought hard. Clearly an answer was expected. One he should get right. Would Sir Asif, young Mr Asif Ibrahim then, have quietly accepted that five-hundred-rupee bribe. Five hundred rupees would have been a considerable amount of money in those distant days. Was this the old man's way of saying that sometimes something wrong is after all irresistible?

He could not see it. It was not possible that the young man who was to become this old man would have accepted that bribe, however easy it might have been to have slipped the large piece of paper, faintly smelling of spices, no doubt, like all hidden-away currency notes, up into his cuff and to have said no more about it. No, Asif Ibrahim then as now would have sent that temptingly huge sum back.

'You returned the basket, Sir Asif.'

'Oh yes, I returned the basket. But I returned it at the hands of my sweeper.'

He felt himself stiffen and jolt back in his chair as if he too had been subjected to that contemptuous insult.

'Yes, Inspector, you do right to purse your lips. It was a thoroughly gratuitous action. And I was proud of it. Proud of it. So much so that I took the earliest opportunity of recounting the whole incident to the Collector, one Brown.' Again he paused. 'And I remember to this day the precise terms of the dressing-down that Brown gave me before telling me that I was never to visit that village again, much less to sit there. Let me tell you just what words he used in summing up.'

'Yes, sir?'

'He said this to me: But, Ibrahim, appalling though your conduct has been, I would rather you had done that and hindered the administration of justice throughout the whole of my District than that you had, by the least hint or inclination, appeared to have accepted anything whatsoever in the way or nature of a bribe.'

And the old man's eyes looked into his with unflinching intent.

CHAPTER XIII

ON HIS BED AGAIN that afternoon – errr-bock went the fan, errr-bock, pause, long pause, then again errr-bock – Ghote lay cursing himself. The point of the Judge's story down in the library had struck him with the unexpectedness of a trodden-on snake rearing up and suddenly sinking its fangs into juicy calf muscle. It had been absurdly innocent of him, he realized now, not to have seen it coming. But he had been so distressed at what he had believed was Sir Asif's imminent surrender that he had gone on waiting for the old man's reminiscence to have exactly the opposite point from what had in fact been its intention.

Yet surely, he thought now, he ought to have known from the very beginning. Sir Asif was proof against bribery of any sort, just as he was proof against blackmail. Neither threatening to tell the world the secret of the old fort nor offering to keep that secret when he ought to have reported it was going to affect that long-matured integrity.

But he had touched the old man. To the depths.

He had been right in his assessment of the situation between them all the way up to the final moments. Sir Asif could not endure the thought of an Ibrahim, of his own son, being confined to – what was the old-fashioned word he had once used? – to a madhouse. Confined with common criminals, criminal lunatics. And he had been near giving way. He had certainly contemplated the possibility. The look on his face had been too plain.

But the possibility had been contemplated, and then stepped back from.

Lunch had been hell, he thought with sudden inconsequence.

His mind went back to the scene. The Judge sitting balefully at the head of the long polished table in the dining-room. Begum Roshan, far away at the opposite end, hands darting and plucking, rushing in with frantic bursts of talk, making fierce declarations quelled abruptly by her father's eye or on a couple of occasions by his tongue, rebukes that might have been addressed to an over-excited child rather than to a woman in full middle age. The Saint, sitting as he always did with feet tucked up under him on the upright, carved, soft-padded dining-chair, and silent. This, too, it appeared, was another day without words and only sunbeam smiles conveyed his feelings. But how they conveyed them, launched into the tension round the table like dowsing buckets of loose earth fanning out on to a creeping fire. Yet the fire had been too deep-seated to be wholly extinguished even by those all-embracing sweeps of radiant benignity. And it was always quite plain, too, from where the tension came. From the Judge.

But he himself had been the only one to know its cause.

The others had been simply the victims of that scalding tongue. Victims each in a different way. Raman, of course, had caught the worst of it. He was the most defenceless. It was the European-style meal that was always presented at midday, brown soup which tasted merely oily, a roast chicken so scrawny that, served plain as it was, it was hard to get down at all, and after that what Raman called, using one of his infrequent, mangled English expressions, 'secon' toast', three little strips of salty tinned fish resting on small squares of oil-sogged toasted bread and distinguished from a non-existent 'first toast' only by coming at the end of the meal instead of at its beginning, and whatever the Orderly did in serving it had been wrong. And had been paid for in blasting words.

He, too, had come in for his share of the plainly scathing whenever, feeling bound to do what he could to create the harmony he had been fundamentally responsible for causing to vanish, he had ventured to put in a word, either into the limping and awkward conversation or into the difficult silence.

In the case of Father Adam, white Naxalite, it had been open warfare. The matter of the bund and its breaching had been at the root of it. Looking back, it was hard to remember exactly how it had been raised. But he was almost certain Sir Asif had said something deliberately which he knew would cause the priest, that invalid here in the house at the request of Cousin Karim in Washington, a guest who could not by the rules of hospitality be asked to leave, to say something in his turn about the bund which would only be objectionable to him. The old man had been punishing himself. Punishing himself for that moment of weakness in the library, that moment of covetousness.

'So you consider then, Father Adam, that a man has no right to the property held by his forefathers for generations?'

'No, of course he hasn't, Judge. Property is theft. We all know that.'

'We know nothing of the kind, sir. What we know is the law. The law as it has been given to us by our legislators. And that law here expressly includes the right to property.'

'Well, Judge, I understood you weren't always in agreement with the wisdom of your legislators, particularly your country's present set-up, if what I read in that thing *The Sputnik* is right.'

'It is perfectly right, sir. Our present Parliament is a disgrace. A disgrace to its predecessors even, and yet more of a disgrace to that Mother of Parliaments at Westminster from which it takes its life.'

'So you're a Britisher rather than an Indian, is that it?'

'I am not, sir. I am an Indian. Born in India. Of unimpeachable Indian ancestry. A man – '

'Except your ancestors arrived in India as blood-bathed

conquerors, isn't that so?'

'Blood-bathed they were not, I'll have you know. You so-called liberals can only think in one mould. You believe that because force exists, and force has to exist in this world of ours, you believe that any person who exercises it must be what you would call a blood-streaked murderer.'

'Oh, I know that force exists all right, Judge. I'm just concerned to see that it's used on the right side for a change.'

'And what might your definition of the right side be? Taking away a man's land to give to a pack of peasants too ignorant to use it properly?'

The priest had leant forward across the table towards Sir Asif then, his tangled eyebrows locked together more fiercely than ever in his dangerously pale face.

'Yes, Judge,' he had answered. 'I believe that to take a far corner of your precious gardens so as to divert a river and bring a better life to hundreds of poverty-stricken individuals is a cause that would certainly justify the use of force. Extreme force if it has to be.'

And the Judge had made no answer. He had cut the dispute off with a long glowering silence. A silence that had underlined, as nothing else might have done, the full import of the priest's declaration.

Yes, priest though he might be – if he was, if he truly was – he was plainly a man prepared to use force to gain ends he believed in. Even extreme force.

Errr-bock. Errr-bock.

All right, fan. Nothing changes, you say. In this sleepy old house. But something may. Something very certainly may. And if the old Judge is killed, fan, then will anyone afterwards stir that ancient generator into life to keep you going round? If you have not stopped of your own accord at last before that.

But the thought of the generator and the long tin shed under the tamarind tree, bleached by season after season of heat like this to a whitish grey to match the whitish green of the desiccated foliage round it, recalled to him that there, hidden in its darkest corner still, were Mr Dhebar's motor-scooter and his own bright, battered, deplorable tan-coloured suitcase.

Better go out quietly now, he thought, and fetch that myself, rather than risk drawing Sir Asif's attention to the way I came back here by asking to have it fetched when the servants are up and about.

He slid off the high bed and got into shirt and trousers, and the chappals he had mercifully changed into before he had begun his vigil in the shed. Thank goodness, too, that his one necktie was still away somewhere in the servants' quarter being ironed into respectability again after its spell of useful work keeping the unconscious boulder-chested Sikander safe until he had been carried back to his underground prison.

Gripping the chappals with extra-careful sweat-sticky toes, he was able to go the length of the tall airless silent passage outside without making more than the slightest of noises.

Around him he could feel the whole old house profoundly sleeping. Sir Asif, a volume of verse from the little bookrack on his bedside teapoy perhaps lying beside him where it had fallen. Begum Roshan, twitching restlessly no doubt in her sleep, but asleep. The Saint, stretched out on the bedcover folded on the hard floor, asleep though and smiling perhaps through his white square of a beard. Father Adam, tangled brows at last unlocked, trumpeting out snores of protest to the unheeding world. Raman, wherever it was that he had his sleeping place in the servants' quarter, free for a while from Sir Asif's battering scoldings and, for a certainty, with that horseshoe grin of his coming and going as he dreamed. Dreamed of what? Of the South and his boyhood, before that killing of his was ever thought of? Of perhaps slowly paddling some lazy boat through jewel-smooth waters and singing like a bird his boating-song? And, somewhere nearby as well, the other servants, deeply and mercifully asleep in the suffocating heat.

The rat colonies, too, in those deserted rooms in the other

wing, they would be smothered in sleep. And the black-striped squirrels in their tree homes in the sun-locked gardens, not one of them would be venturing in now at a broken-shuttered window to finish as a little baked corpse in a long-deserted bedroom.

And down at the far end of the gardens, under the ruin of the old fort, Sikander, would he too be sleeping? Or would he be raging still, the madman recaptured, hurling himself at his bars?

Going down the wide wooden staircase with its elaborate carved banisters, he was conscious that his chappals were flipping and flapping a little more loudly. But he still felt confident that no one in the big sleeping house would stir at the sound.

At the stairs' foot he crept, more silently again, over to the tall outer doors and let himself out into the full glare of the implacable sun. He blinked and shook his head. His uniform cap or the sunglasses which he seldom felt a need for in Bombay would have been a blessing. But they could be done without.

He moved off into the dusty parched garden. Within a few paces sweat had sprung up all over him. Within a few paces more it had dried right away again. He walked steadily on, following what must have been the exact path he had taken in the darkness when he had crept after the white shape of Raman's neat jacket as the Orderly had carried Sikander sahib his evening meal.

How long ago that seemed. Time, under the deadening heat, seemed to stretch and stretch here.

There was little shade to be had on the way with the sun high in the whitened sky above. No shrub now in this dry heat gave out more than the most grudging of odours.

Ahead the outline of the ruined fort was black against the horizon. But not to be looked at long. Best, with that enemy there above never slackening in his bombardment, to keep eyes down to the ground. Which glared back enough in any case.

And now, at last, the shed. Lift the tin door and hold it up as it swung open. Nobody perhaps to hear its squealing grate on the iron-hard earth underneath, but better to be safe. Say it disturbed Sikander and he launched himself into a bout of howling that penetrated to the outside air, possibly woke an anxious Sir Asif, caused him to rout out Raman . . .

Inside the shed it was at least a different sort of heat. Not the blasting assault of the direct sun but a thick and smelly mugginess, the confined odour of old oil slowly drying in the baking warmth, of metal at a temperature too hot for hand to bear, of battery acid evaporating drop by drop. And it was dark, thickly dark, but hardly coolly dark.

He groped his way with difficulty past the generator itself, then past the high bank of big old batteries, and finally past the fuel tank, to where, hardly to be seen, Mr Dhebar's scooter stood where he had pushed it at dawn, with beside it the suitcase.

It was going to be even hotter work lugging the damn thing all the way back.

But it ought to be done.

True, he had put Sir Asif heavily in his debt by saving Raman from that ravening man-turned-beast. But he still needed every ounce, every half-gramme, of goodwill that he could levy from the old man. Because he had lost a lot of ground with his attempt at bribery. No doubt of that. Though the Judge had rejected his offer in what was, for him, the gentlest possible way, it was still plain that in that implacable scale of virtues he had slid far down again. So to draw attention to himself now by this appalling reminder of his not-so-distant expulsion from the house in disgrace would be stupid indeed. Worth a lot of toil under the broiling sun to avoid that.

He gave himself a few minutes' rest and then picked up the wretched case and lugged it out of the shed, set it down again, closed the tin door with an effort, picked up his burden once more and set off. At once the licking sun dried up all the profuse sweat that had beaded itself on him in the sticky darkness of the shed.

Back along the now all too familiar dry-dusty path, changing the awkward weight from one stretched arm to the other every ten yards or so, feeling the beat of that distant, incredibly powerful heat-source now like a red iron pressed throbbingly on the back of his neck.

By the time he reached the house again and leant against the wide doors to push them open, his head was swimming as if there was a heavy ball inside it bouncing from side to side in great irregular swoops and his eyes were pricking as if they had been slow!y poached in steamy water over a hot brazier.

He heaved the case inside and let it flop down. It made a flumping sound that, half an hour before when he had crept out, would have made him curse himself to ribbons. Yet now he could not care.

But he rested there just inside the blissful comparative cool of the house, waiting nevertheless to hear whether the noise had roused any of the sleeping inhabitants.

And it was then that there came another sound. One he had not in the least expected to hear. The unmistakable tap-tap-tap of the keys of a typewriter being slowly and laboriously operated.

He could hardly believe his ears.

Yet the sound was beyond denying that of typewriter keys. Though it was not easy to make out just where it was coming from. The high echoing passages converging on the central hall with its big mounting carved staircase was not the easiest of places for accurately locating sounds.

But how splendid that the sound was there. Someone typing at this dead hour of the heat-stifled day could be only someone typing in secret. Could be only the person who had sent the threatening notes to Sir Asif.

So catch them. Work out just where the sound was coming from. Find it at all costs. Creep up. Fling open a door and see then someone – Who would it be? Which of them? – bending over a typewriter, a large white sheet of paper rolled into it in front of them, laboriously tapping out another message. Step into that room and say that the plot, the piece of mischief, the coldly intended murder plan was at an end.

And it would be over, this whole burdensome business. Done. Finished. Sir Asif would be out of danger and all would be well. He would be able to leave. To go back to Bombay, and its everyday bustle.

He licked quickly at his dry lips and set out towards the nearest passage, digging sweaty toes furiously into the old leather of his chappals, picking the soles right up to his heels so that they made not the least sound on the wide cracked marble floor.

But he had barely gone five yards when it became clear that he had chosen wrongly. The tap-tap-tapping, slow and painstaking, the work of an amateur typist – but which of them would not be that? – had died almost completely to nothingness.

Rapidly he retraced his steps, his heart thudding at the prospect of the tapping having died away because the message being typed had been finished.

But no.

Back in the hall beside the bulky shape of his suitcase the little distant click-clicking was once more clearly audible.

He set off in the opposite direction, going yet more rapidly this time, a little less careful about keeping his chappals from making any sound.

And in this passage, the one marked by the map of Bangladesh in mildew, the laborious tap-tapping was not dying away. It was gradually growing louder.

He crept along towards it, caution once more restored. No doubt the person working at that secret task would not be quite careless of any possible interruption. No doubt half their attention at least would be on any possible sound coming from outside whichever room it was they were at work in. Perhaps it was this that accounted for the slowness of the tapping. If, say, the culprit was the American, who might be expected to be almost a born typewriter-user, then it might be just the need to listen out that was making that moment by moment louder-growing sound so slow and laborious.

But the next waited-for click had failed to come. The sound was no longer going on.

For a moment he stopped just where he was, over-whelmed by spiralling-down dismay. But he forced himself to thrust it aside. The clicking had been coming from somewhere ahead. Silence did not mean he had chosen the wrong approach altogether. In fact it was almost certain now that the typewriter itself was in one of the rooms just round the corner in front of him, those smaller rooms he had searched when he had been looking for signs of a hidden extra member of the household, the rooms that had fallen out of use. Any one of them would be an excellent choice for typing a message in secret.

Only, if he had got his geography right, the passage ahead round the corner led on to the kitchen quarter. So it would have a way of escape. Not an easy one for the American, or even perhaps for the Saint. But a lot more practical for Begum Roshan.

He abandoned his stealth and went forward at a loping, clacking run. He reached the corner. The narrower passage ahead was empty. And the tap-tap-tapping still had not started up again.

Only one thing for it. He swung round and hurled wide the nearest door. One rapid glance into the room beyond. Empty. White-shrouded furniture, the air so undisturbed he could almost have poked a hole in it.

He swung away. Ran to the next door, crashed it open. And again heavy tranquillity. Not a sign of any human being. Nor of a being having been there.

Quick, the next room. Stride, stride, stride along the passage. Seize the knob of the door, jerk it round, fling the door wide. And –

And, clear to see in the diffused light coming in through

gaps in the closed shutters, a small square table under the window with its white sheeting thrown back. And on the table a typewriter. A tall old-fashioned office typewriter.

But no sheet of paper rolled into it. And no one bent over it laboriously typing. No one.

CHAPTER XIV

FOR A LONG MOMENT Ghote stood furiously devouring with his eyes the sight of the typewriter standing there on the square table under the room's shuttered window. Surely he must be able to learn something from it. Not two minutes earlier, scarcely one, someone had been striking at those keys. Not two minutes earlier there had been a sheet of white paper rolled in there. On it would have been typed words, the words beyond doubt of yet another note threatening with death Justice Sir Asif Ibrahim, pronouncer of the Madurai sentences.

But nothing was left of the presence that had been there. Not a trace remained of the evil thoughts that had been directed like jabs from a ray gun at the narrow gap where the machine's keys had one by one struck.

Oh yes, there would be fingerprints on those keys which the fleeing writer would have had no time meticulously to wipe off. There might even have been fingerprints there from all the times the machine had been used before for the other notes, fingerprints that would have been there for him to have found earlier if a proper search of the whole huge house had been in any way a practical proposition. But that would have been a task for a team of ten, at the very least.

And if this had been the proper world of Bombay instead of this world-to-itself, cut off from everything, then it would have been a simple matter to have impounded the machine, sent it to the Fingerprint Bureau under seal and to have got comparison prints from all the suspects. The

affair would have been wrapped up in hours. Then. But this
was not Bombay. By the time the typewriter had been
delivered there, by heaven knows what route, it would in all
probability be too late. The time for the Judge would have
come and gone.

The thoughts ran through his mind in rapid this-way-and-
that jerks. By the ticking hand of a watch they lasted no
more than two or three seconds.

And then he had wheeled round, was pounding out of the
stuffy shadowed little room, had swung in the direction of
the kitchen quarter, was pelting full speed towards it.

That unseen figure had stopped typing less than two
minutes before. It would be perfectly possible to catch
them up, however fast they were running with that thick
sheet of white paper clutched in one hand.

There was a bead curtain at the far end of the passage.
He charged through it.

But his quickly darting eyes found no one on the other
side, only the passage running onwards. Its walls here were
no longer white-plastered but left in their natural reddish
clay colour, and all along the tops of them ran broad wooden
shelves storing boxes and bottles and cartons and net-bags,
crammed so closely together that there was no room for
anyone, however slight in build, to have hidden there.

He ran past.

At the far end came the kitchen itself. A big bare room, a
smouldering fire under its wide chimney making the already
hot and unmoving air all the more burningly sultry. Round
the walls in nets and in round wire cages hung yet more
provisions. In clumps on the floor there rested the age-old
implements of cookery, dozens of round iron degshas varying
in size from no more than a cup to ones big as cauldrons, the
heavy stone slab of a pata, with on it the round rolling
vaniata, a big board for slapping out puris and chapattis, a
large round iron mortar, its heavy iron pestle leaning inside
it. Only one object in the whole big room indicated that this
was not any time in the past two or three hundred years: a tall

old refrigerator near the far corner.

As he came to a halt, looking wildly round for any sign of a human presence, the machine gave a groaning shudder and throbbed angrily as its motor worked. A wild thought came to him. He sprinted across and tugged open the tall door.

But neither the Saint, saffron-garbed and white-bearded, nor the American priest, casually dressed, tangled of eyebrow, was standing there shivering. Only rack-like shelves with pots and jars and basins higgeldy-piggeldy on them, milk, cooling juice from the tamarind tree, a solid block of ice-cream-like kulfi on a blue plate, the remains of what they had had at dinner on that first night, other lumps and liquids less easy to guess at.

He slowly pushed the door to. And then he saw there was a human presence in the big room after all. From the narrow gap between the tall machine and the corner, two dusty-soled feet and two skinny ankles protruded at floor level.

Was this the Saint? Had he dived crouching for cover there? It could not be that white Naxalite. It could not be Begum Roshan. She had silver rings on her toes.

It was Raman. He was lying, fast asleep, curled up on a cloth he had spread in this corner, perhaps a quarter of a degree cooler than elsewhere. His eyes were firmly closed. He was breathing deeply, on the verge of snoring. But on his face there was no sudden-come horseshoe grin to show that he was dreaming, dreaming of poling a boat through jewel-calm, green-shaded waters.

Leave him to lie. There was an archway at the opposite corner of the smoke-tickling room. The typewriter user must have gone through it. The search in here had taken only seconds.

He pelted over.

Beyond the arch there was another room, another store-place with heavier, more substantial items stacked against its walls in tubs and crates and gunny sacks, knobbly or bulging. A rapid glance round convinced him that here too there was nowhere anyone could hide. But there was a door at the

appalling sun. My dear sir, I have walked all the way from the village, from where the weekly bus deposited me.'

Looking at him, he saw that what he had said bore all the marks of truth. His feet were dust-caked, the bottom of his dhoti was more red than white, and his shoulders were sagging much as his own had done after he had lugged his heavy case up from the generator shed. More even.

So was it certain that the fellow had not been inside the house at the time that typewriter had been used? But he might have made his way up from the village half an hour earlier, going through the gardens when he himself had been inside the generator shed nerving himself up for the trek back. And, if that was what had happened, then to lie at once and stick to the lie would be the only course open to the fellow.

He cursed himself for not having put his questions in a more roundabout way. But it was too late now, though he would do what he could.

He coughed. 'But was it not you I glimpsed just a few minutes ago?' he asked. 'Coming out of a room on the way to the kitchen quarter?'

'Oh no, no, my dear sir. Would that I had been inside there. In the shade. In the blessed shade.'

'But what are you doing here in any case?'

'My dear Doctor, my motor-scooter.'

He felt a twinge of shame. Not once had he thought about how the editor, who after all had been unusually kind, was going to get his machine back.

'Ah yes, your scooter, of course,' he said. 'Well, it is all right. It is in a safe place. A thoroughly safe place. I have put it in that shed with the generator motor. You know where that is?'

'Down at the far end of the gardens beside the fort,' Mr Dhebar said, casting a sad glance over the long sun-battered stretch of baked earth between him and the distant tamarind tree.

'Yes, yes, it is there. But surely you do not need to have

the machine straight away? You can come inside and rest. Raman will get you some cold water.'

The editor perked up at the suggestion.

'Ah yes,' he said. 'Inside. Inside. That would be excellent. Yes, to rest indoors for a little. For some time even. To take a drink of water. Perhaps even to stay until tea is served. To take tea here. From the hand of Begum Roshan. That would make all my travail worthwhile indeed.'

A small signal flag seemed to flick up inside him.

'But this travail of yours?' he asked with a new sharpness. 'What for did you undertake it? What for did you come all this way in the heat? Did you have some sudden need for your scooter?'

'Yes,' said Mr Dhebar, jumping like some fat fish for a gobbet of food. 'Yes, a sudden need. Most important.'

'But then why is it you now intend to remain until tea is served? That is a good time away.'

'I – I – er. That is to say, I . . .'

'Yes?' he asked.

He stood under the unvarying glaze of the sun, four-square in front of the dumpy figure of the editor, and waited for an answer.

Mr Dhebar licked his thick, dry lips.

'Well,' he said, 'it is difficult to explain.'

'Explain, please, nevertheless.'

His stand was so unyielding that clearly it never occurred to Mr Dhebar that he could simply say that he was not going to account for his action, however inconsistent it might seem, to a mere Doctor of Philosophy. He just stood there patently striving to find some convincing answer.

And when at last it came it was not what he had expected.

'Doctor . . . Doctor, there is something that perhaps I should tell you. It is something that I did not think I would ever tell. Until the time. Until it became a matter of common knowledge.'

He waited for him. There was no need to press or prompt any more. It had been begun: the rest would follow.

The sun was like an unrelenting screw on the top of his head.

'Doctor, you know me. I am an educated fellow. A graduate, Doctor. Second class honours, nearly first. I am the editor of a journal of opinion.' A dry strangled cough. 'But I know where I came from. And I know how far I will be able to go. I believe I have done well for myself. I know that I have. As well perhaps as I could have done. But – but Sir Asif – '

A check.

From the moment he had felt, somewhere inside, at the level where feelings say more than any amount of careful reasoning, that what Mr Dhebar was going to tell him would take a solid place in his inquiries, his interest had been at a constant high point. But now it went shooting up, like the mercury in a thermometer taken from the coolest place indoors out into the beating sun.

Sir Asif, the fellow had said. And then he had checked himself, appalled by what he evidently saw ahead.

But there would be no turning back still. Not now that what the fellow had to say had been advanced into up to this point. All his experiences of hearing men confess, confess sometimes to the ugliest of crimes, told him that.

So he waited once more. And once more Mr Dhebar went on talking.

'Doctor, Sir Asif Ibrahim is as far above my humble person as Kanchenjunga itself is above the very foothills. Doctor, I am going to marry Sir Asif's daughter.'

If the editor had thought that he would surprise him by what he had said, his expectations were fully justified.

He stood simply staring at him.

Abruptly the hammering sun started up a throbbing ache just above and behind his eyes.

So Mr Dhebar was proposing to cross the line. The line that had once been drawn, deep as a trench, between Begum Roshan and that Hindu lawyer from the South. The line that had been drawn, little doubt about it, by Sir

Asif himself, with the full backing in those distant days of society. And even now, though there were inter-caste marriages enough and inter-community marriages, it was still not at all an easy thing to do, to cross that line.

And at once a lot of things that the editor of *The Sputnik* had said and done fell into a pattern. The fellow's wallowing delight in such ordinary courtesies as Begum Roshan had extended to him. The way the night before that he himself had been admitted to the *Sputnik* office as soon as he had mentioned Begum Roshan's name. The very remarks the fellow had made after he had told the story of Begum Roshan's proposed marriage and how it had come to nothing. All that stuff about things today not being as they were. And then there were the hours and hours he must have spent wading through the stiffening pages of those dusty files of *The Hindu* to discover the details of that story. And finally there was the readiness with which he had agreed to lend at a moment's notice his valuable motor-scooter, with no good reason given.

And now . . . Now he must have come out all the way here, not of course simply to re-claim that machine, but to seek as soon as he could Begum Roshan's gratitude for what he had done in her name. No wonder he had seemed so delighted at the prospect of staying solemnly to take tea on the terrace with Sir Asif and his daughter.

And his daughter. But would Sir Asif, proud Sir Asif, who had recounted once with no misgivings the ruthless exploits of his family in bygone days, would he ever allow his only daughter to marry the jumped-up little editor he so manifestly despised? Would the man who had prevented her marriage with an up-and-coming young lawyer simply because he was a Hindu allow another Hindu, by no means up-and-coming, to marry her now?

Not over his dead body.

And so – he turned away and began to walk towards the house and its shade – was this man here with him now, in his heavily pleated dhoti, with his solid belly and his deter-

mined pear-heavy jaw, was he coldly setting about a scheme
to scare the aged Judge to death? Or, failing that, was he
planning to kill him so that he could marry the heir to this
big old house? So that he could inherit it all, its treasures, its
land, its influence?

It was possible. It was distinctly possible. But it was not
proved.

CHAPTER XV

GHOTE PRECEDED Mr Dhebar towards the high, powdery-
white bulk of the house and its promise of shade, if not of
coolness. No need, he knew, to march along beside him. The
battering sun would get him indoors as effectively as if he
was surrounded by a guard of rifle-carrying Armed Police.
But, once inside, he would keep the fellow in sight.

Now he knew him to have such a motive for at the least
forcing the Judge into a position where he would be unable
to object to this marriage with Begum Roshan, he would
have to watch over him like a kite once he had a new opportunity of advancing his scheme by leaving yet another
note for Sir Asif to find, a note typed out on a machine
which would not necessarily implicate him as the typewriter
in the *Sputnik* office would.

But he was not to get out of the heat as soon as he had
hoped. When he was within two or three paces of the thin
band of shadow which the looming bulk of the house was
now beginning to cast, his eye was caught by a movement
somewhere in the gardens behind him.

It was not rapid, but any movement in that deadened sun-
blasted vista attracted attention. For a few moments he was
unable to make out just what it was. He stood squinting
against the glare, half feeling he was being a fool to stop and
look.

But then he saw it. It was a saffron-coloured shape,

hardly visible behind a straggling clump of leafily overgrown oleanders, moving at a quiet and steady pace away from him.

The Saint.

The Saint, too, out here in the gardens. There was, of course, no reason why he should not be. Yet it was the time of day when everybody who was able to got themselves into the coolest place they could – even under an ancient in-effective fan, errr-bock, errr-bock, errr-bock – and stayed there asleep or at least lying still until the worst was over. And it was an undeniable fact that, not so very long before, someone had been typing there inside the house and had stopped abruptly and hurried out, out here into the gardens.

So perhaps after all Mr Dhebar had been telling the simple truth when he had said that he had not been inside the house. Perhaps, for all his admitted ambition to marry Sir Asif Ibrahim's daughter, he was not the person leaving the threatening notes. Yet perhaps he was. Perhaps he had such a note on his person now and was hoping for a chance to deliver it unobserved.

What to do?

Mr Dhebar was still coming up towards the house, walking a good deal more slowly than he himself had done. As if he had indeed just tramped all the way from the village under the broiling sun. He looked as if all that he would do once he had got indoors was to collapse on to the nearest seat and sit there hoping to be brought a cooling drink.

And the Saint was moment by moment getting further away.

He squared his shoulders and set off once again through the pulsating heat.

The Saint, he saw, was some hundred and fifty yards distant, walking quite slowly, white-crowned unprotected head held high, apparently oblivious of the pounding sun.

He forced himself to stride out. And before very long he saw that the direction in which the two of them were heading would bring them eventually to the little hillock on which was outlined, trembling a little to the eye in the heat, the ruin of the old fort.

So the Saint was out here, in all probability, not because he had just been chased out of the house with an incriminating sheet of typed paper on his person, but because he was going to visit the disciple he had possessed in those long ago days when it had seemed so important that the British should be expelled for ever from India's shores.

Would it be worth trying to overhear what these two said to each other? Or should he turn and hurry back to the house in case after all Mr Dhebar was not as exhausted as he looked, was even now prowling determinedly about looking for a chance to leave a new threat to Sir Asif?

The headache which had started when he had first confronted the editor had become a real stinker now, jabbing from inside at eyeballs and eardrums with an implacable regular beat.

It was possible that what the Saint would have to say to mad Sikander, his one time disciple, would have no bearing at all on the mysteries that lay concealed, like so many rats' nests, in the slow life of the big house starkly white behind him. It was possible. But the chances were that, in such an intimate discussion between two people who had known the house and its ways so long, something would be said that would cast some light into the shadowed places.

And surely Mr Dhebar had looked really exhausted. Surely.

He took the decision, tried with dry tongue to moisten parched mouth, and hurried onwards. The air seemed hot as the fumes of a fire.

Ahead the Saint was walking steadily towards his objective, saffron robes hanging heavily from him in the stillness. When at last he reached the little outcrop on which the ruin was perched, he mounted the earthen steps set here and there into it at the same unvarying pace, as if he was still progressing over the level dusty ground of the rest of the gardens.

Halting in the shelter of the generator shed just where before under moonlight he had seen Raman finish his journey with the draped food tray, he watched the saffron-clad figure make his way with practised steps round to where the narrow entrance slit to the fort lay and disappear.

The moment that saffron-clad shape had gone, he made his own way quickly forward, taking the slope of the little hill at something approaching a run and flattening himself at once against the nearest wind-eroded pinkish wall of the ruin.

Then he sidled round as quickly as he could to the slit-like doorway, back flat against the heat-throbbing stones. There he stood and listened with all his might. Soon, above the tiny subdued leg-rubbing squeaks of insects the sun had brought to life, he thought he could make out the sound of the Saint's bare feet slap-slapping their way along the tunnel immediately below.

He counted to ten, slowly as he could force himself to, and then slipped into the entrance.

The darkness after the white glare outside was like a wall in front of him. But now quite clearly he could hear the Saint's bare feet progressing steadily away from him. He set himself to descend one by one the twelve deep steps he knew to be there, little though he could see them.

When he found he had reached the bottom he stopped to listen again, and as soon as he had satisfied himself that the Saint was making his way steadily on towards the barred gate of Sikander's prison, he began to make his own way forward, hands held outwards so that, as before, his fingertips just scraped the sticky bat-smeared walls to either side.

At last he came to the corner where, when he had been here before, he had first seen the dim light that had told him definitely that there was someone hidden down in this sharply stinking darkness. And, though he had wondered whether after Sikander's escape he would still see that dim glow, it was there again. And outlined against it he could make out the bulky robed form of the Saint.

He stepped back round past the corner again and then squatted low and put his head round once more. Like that, he calculated, he would have no difficulty in hearing what was said at the barred gate while, if the innocent Saint should chance unexpectedly to turn round, he would be reasonably hard to see in the dark.

If anything was said. If the silence-vowed Saint was going to speak at all.

And it seemed that he was not. Instead of calling out to Sikander, by way of announcing himself he simply ran his fingers along the iron bars of the gate till they gave out a low musical ringing.

But the sound seemed to produce no answer. Was Sikander no longer here? Or could he be sleeping? Or, perhaps, most likely, was he sulking in the depths of his lair, still broodingly furious at the failure of his escape?

The Saint, however, appeared to be altogether unperturbed by this lack of response. After half a minute or so he gently lowered himself to the ground until he was seated cross-legged on the tunnel floor facing the cell. Then, leaning a little forward, he resumed his musical twanging along the bars. Before long the whole narrow passage was ringing with the sound.

And then, with a suddenness made all the more shocking by its contrast with the soft musical hum in the air all round, there came the crash of sheer animal noise that he had heard down here once before, and the madman was at the locked gate again, jerking and bounding and attacking the bars as if once more he was going to root them out of the solid stone and all the while yelling with the full force of his massive boulder-broad chest.

The noise racketed past him, wave on wave, till, as had happened when he too had confronted that raging imprisoned thing, there began at last to be a slackening.

Now he waited to hear, at last, the Saint's voice.

But no sound overrode the animal moaning that Sikander's rage had descended to.

And soon he recognized that no sound was going to come. The Saint's vow held here in the darkness, with no one but the madman to hear, as firmly as it held in the stiff social world of the house.

But he knew that in the dim light the seated cross-legged figure at the bars was communicating with the creature behind them as surely as earlier communication had taken place between Sikander and himself. The Saint, he guessed, was smiling, smiling his smile from within his square of white full-falling beard like the implacable sun itself. Only not an enemy to be shunned. Instead a force that warmed, warmed to the depths, penetrating, melting.

Yet Sikander now began to rage again. The sound of his tearaway screams mounting and mounting in the close confines of the darkness.

Easy to imagine the contorted face, the working muscles, the impression that behind the grimaces and the writhing there was nothing but a blindly directed will wanting only destruction. Was it too strong then for that smiling force he himself had experienced and succumbed to?

Perhaps not. The raging fit did not this time last very long. And the seated figure this side of the bars did not budge by so much as an inch.

For minute after minute down in the almost complete bat-stinking darkness the battle between the two elemental forces continued. But it was not long before it became clear that the smile of the Saint was in the ascendant. Each time Sikander heaved and rattled at his bars the assault was less loud. Each time he yelled and screamed he did so with less conviction.

Kneeling at the tunnel's corner, he watched fascinated as the contest wore on, oblivious of strained limbs, gradually losing even his pounding headache.

And at last Sikander, plainly, became entirely quiet. Would the Saint speak now? Would he, for the sake of this demented being, release himself from his arid self-imposed vow?

The silence grew. Once more he was able to make out from somewhere further inside the underground dwelling-place the sound, so slight that it seemed only to caress his eardrums, of a tiny trickling of water.

And still there came no break in the silence. The Saint sat unmoving, and on the other side of the barred door, becoming with the passing minutes easier and easier to see, stood the chastened madman.

It was the latter who at last spoke. A low, quiet voice speaking in English, good English, and easy to hear in the stone-surrounded silence.

'So you have come again, my old friend?'

He did not expect the greeting to be answered, and it was not. Or not in words.

'Well, are you going to tell me nothing again this time? Nothing? Not a word about the damned . . .'

Sikander's voice had begun to climb up in volume and ferocity. But it rapidly tailed off. It was not difficult to imagine the smile that had quenched its first angry glint of flame.

'But it still goes on out there, doesn't it? It still goes on. The oppression. The injustice. So many long years of fighting it and nothing achieved. Nothing.'

Speak, he willed the silent seated figure at the far end of the tunnel. Speak. Tell him. Explain. Now that he is quiet, now that he will listen, tell him. Tell him that he need not rage any more. Tell him the days of the British oppression are long past. That it is all over. That India is free. Free and proud.

He checked himself.

There were things it would be wrong to ask a truth-dedicated saint to say. But surely, surely, he could at least tell this poor demented creature that the British days had finished. That India was, for better or worse, free. That the force that had driven him mad was no longer there.

Surely that was the least any one human being could do for another?

But the Saint neither spoke nor moved.

And before he himself could give way to the rash temptation rapidly growing up in him and announce, shout out, the good news, Sikander began to speak again.

'Well, the only thing left is to fight on. To fight on and on. And if they won't let me fight with a gun, fight with dynamite, fight with a sword even, then I will have to fight with paper. My friend, will you take another Memorial for me? Will you? It's our only hope now, to appeal to the King Emperor. And perhaps he is a just man, perhaps.' The lamenting voice paused, and then resumed. 'Old friend, if I compose another Memorial, will you come back tomorrow and take it to deliver? Will you? Will you?'

There came no answer. Or not in words. But even from the distance he could see on the face of the madman that the Saint had responded to his plea. Had responded, of course, with a smile. A smile that had said 'Yes'.

He decided it was time to retreat. The Saint had visited the wreck of the man who had once been his follower, his follower in war, not one of his many, many followers in peace of today, and he had agreed to the request made to him. He had come and he had brought a little peace. In all probability he would end his visit now.

And if he turned round it was not impossible, for a man with his powers, that he would spot him at once, dark though it was, might see him even through the stone walls after he had backed away round the corner.

He rose swiftly to his feet, fighting stiffness, and made his way quickly as he could back along the narrow, dark, stinking, bat-slimy tunnel to the steps and daylight.

And the blaze of the sun again.

But there had been no point in staying, he reflected as he made his way down from the fort's outcrop and into the dusty baked gardens. He had learnt plenty.

The fact was that the madman down there – God, the sun was hot, dizzying and dazzling, but he must hurry – was in communication with the world outside. He was, for a fact, doing what Raman had vaguely talked of him as doing, 'memboralizing', writing letters. And perhaps down there somewhere he had a typewriter for his own use, a toy to keep the madman happily occupied. And so it might well be that somehow he was tricking the Saint into sending threatening letters to his own father, or even begging him to take them. Letters containing death threats.

It seemed unlikely on the face of it that a person like the Saint would agree to such an activity. But it might be. Saints, never forget, operate on a different logic. It might be that Anand Baba would see no reason why Sir Asif should not be threatened. It might even be that he would see no reason why Sir Asif's life here on earth should not come to an end. On the thirtieth anniversary of the Madurai sentences. It might be. It might be.

CHAPTER XVI

IT WAS STILL well before the time that, with the first hint of a slackening in the full heat of the sun, the big, still house would begin to stir to life again when Ghote at last stepped back into its shade out of the pulsation of the glare. He saw at once that his monstrosity of a suitcase was still where he had let it flop down – how long ago was it? – when he had returned with it from its hiding-place in the generator shed and had heard that sudden hope-giving sound of a typewriter being used somewhere in the house. Tap, tap, tap.

He sighed.

Certainly he had missed that gods-given chance. But his time out under the full blast of the afternoon sun had not been entirely wasted after all. He had learnt an unexpected fact about the madman locked underneath the fort which had given him a whole new possibility to work on. And he had found Mr Dhebar, too, found him prowling in the gardens, if prowling was not too strong a word for that dejected tramp of his.

Should he go at once and make sure where the editor

was? Make sure, as far as he still could, that he had not planted another threatening note for Sir Asif to find when he woke from his afternoon sleep?

Or had he not better get the damned suitcase up to the safety of his room before Sir Asif could see it and be reminded of his guest's earlier appalling behaviour?

Yes, perhaps a quick trip upstairs.

He heaved up the case and, leaning a little to one side, head hanging, he set off quietly as he could up the wide carved staircase.

And then in the heat-deadened silence he heard from the head of the stairs above him the unmistakable sound of firm descending steps, the steps of someone wearing shoes.

He looked up, caught in the act, unmentionable suitcase hanging heavily from his stretched arm. It was Father Adam, mystery priest, white Naxalite.

He forced himself into calmness.

'Good afternoon, Father,' he said.

'Mort. Mort. You ought to call me Mort, old buddy.'

'Yes. Yes, of course. I am always inclined to forget. You must excuse our altogether formal Indian manners – er – Mort.'

'They're just a sign, buddy boy.'

He knew he should not ask what they were just a sign of. To begin with, he vaguely suspected he knew the answer already. And, secondly, if he said nothing more it was possible he could just walk past without any remarks being made about his suitcase and why he was carrying it.

'What are they a sign of, please, our Indian manners?'

'Of the hidebound Indian mind, bud. Of subservience to a set of outdated social customs inherited from a conqueror race, and, essentially, of economic dependence on the bourgeois ethic.'

He wanted to say, 'Of all that?' But formal Indian good manners prevented him.

'Well, yes,' he answered instead, 'I suppose that is a point of view which can be held, though, to tell the truth, I do not altogether understand.'

'India doesn't altogether understand. That's the whole trouble, buddy boy. And what are you lugging that terrible valise upstairs for? Aren't there any servants around?'

He felt how unfair it was. The fellow should not have even noticed the suitcase. And a Naxalite priest, surely, should not think about servants. He should go about being proud to carry his own burdens, and irritatingly expect others to do so too.

And if the man was up and about now, dressed and wearing shoes, was it not possible that he had been up and about earlier, up and about using a typewriter down in that shadowy, stuffy little room below?

As much to save himself from any further embarrassing remarks as to find the answer to the question that had come into his mind, he shot out a query in his turn.

'But you yourself, what is it you are doing up and about at this extremely hot hour of the day, Mort?'

He was proud of the 'Mort'. He had managed to tack it on in a way that was almost casual. But he wished he had phrased what he had asked more skilfully. The fellow could easily concoct some sort of reply to a question so directly put.

But it seemed that the American could not. He simply stood where he was on the broad stair above and said nothing.

Had he, by a lucky thrust, tumbled him off his seemingly secure perch at just the moment he had thought himself firm and safe?

At last a halting sort of answer came. 'A book. Yeah, I was fresh out of anything to read, and I thought there might possibly be something down there in the library.'

An unlikely story.

He pushed hard again. 'But surely you must know very well, Mort, what is on the shelves in the library? Law books and volumes of verse in Urdu.'

And once more the priest, the Naxalite, looked disconcerted. He was getting him on the run.

But suddenly the white Naxalite relaxed. A smile came on

to his face and the tangle of dark interlocked hair at his eyebrows loosened.

'I guess you got me, Ganesh,' he said.

For one moment, for one quarter-second, against all the evidence, he thought he was going to hear a confession. Just where they were, with a broad flight of the ancient wooden stairs between them. But he knew that the admission had been altogether too off-hand to be the preliminary to a confession to anything at all serious.

'Got you?' he prompted. 'Please?'

The priest smiled again. 'Yup. I have to confess to a sin.'

Can it be, he thought. Can it be, after all? Is it possible that this fellow – really if he is a priest then he should not be – takes the uttering of death threats so lightly that he can smile as he confesses to making them? Certainly he had often before spoken of sin as if it was something that no longer mattered, but is he going to joke about this? Joke about it?

'Well?' he said, stiffly and even sternly.

But the priest did not at once admit to his sin. Instead he took a couple of easy steps down the stairs towards him and then leant backwards against the carved banister in an attitude of extreme casualness.

'You know, Ganesh,' he said, 'I can remember when I was a kid – you know, I was brought up in a very Catholic home, very God-fearing, very pious – well, I can remember that there was one thing I was really scared to do, scared even to think of doing it. I guess I was an average sort of kid and I never cared too much about things like telling lies. You know, I'd go to confession and if I remembered I'd tell the priest and then I'd say my penance and that'd be the end of it. God, the Church was behind the times in those days. Way behind. But there was this one thing.'

But now came an abrupt halt.

Standing, looking up, listening, he realized that, despite the fellow's air of ease, this 'one thing', whatever it was, was something that worried him still. He waited in silence for him to break the barrier that had so suddenly loomed up in front of him.

At last he did. 'Well,' he said with another smile, a slightly lopsided smile. 'Well, it was masturbating, I guess. I mean I'd got it into my head that that was what they meant by the sin against the Holy Ghost. You know, they used to say that that was the one sin that even God could not forgive. Well, I'd gotten myself into a rare old state about that. I wanted to do it. I wanted like hell to do it. But I thought, "God sees me, sees me at it just once, and that's it, it's the end. There'll never be any hope for me then. It'll be Hell gaping wide, whatever I do all the rest of my life." '

Very well, very well, he thought, but there have been plenty of boys believing something like that. Change for change he had known childhood companions who had got themselves into much the same state, not with such a watchful Christian God looking down at them, but much the same. So why was Father Adam telling him all this now? What connection had it got with the fact that the fellow had been going about the empty heat-smothered house like that?

'Yes, yes?' he said, allowing his impatience to show.

The American grinned again. 'Heck,' he said. 'There came the day when I just did it. I thought, "I'm going to, maybe the ceiling'll split wide right over me and a thunderbolt come down, but I'm going to do it." And I did. And the ceiling stayed just the way it was. And the earth kept on turning just the way it had for millions of years. And I slowly began to realize that there was no black, black line drawn anywhere. I guess that afternoon there back in Boston was what made me see the truth of situation ethics, though no one had even invented the term then.'

Again there came a sideways smile, a little deprecating, not a little attractive.

'Please, what are situation ethics?'

The priest looked sharply surprised. 'You don't know, and you're a Doctor of Philosophy?'

He felt a hot flush of shame, sticky and clammy on

the inside edge of his knees.

'Well, yes,' he said in haste. 'Yes, of course I am knowing. It is just – it is just that in India we are calling them the ethics of situation.'

Would the lie pass?

It would.

'Well,' the American said, 'all that's a long way round, I guess, to explain that I was on my way to steal, as a guest in the house.'

'To steal? What to steal?' He felt almost totally bewildered.

But the priest, coming trotting down the stairs now, simply gave him a rueful grin.

'To steal from the ice-box in the kitchen,' he said. 'That ice-cream stuff. What d'you call it? Kulfi. Just can't resist it.'

And with swift-scissoring khaki-clad legs the priest – could he be a priest, after what he had said? – went rapidly past him, down the remaining stairs and off in the direction of the kitchen quarter.

He stood where he was, feeling distinctly dazed.

What had all that meant? Had the man been telling the simple truth? Did the simple truth mean anything to a man like that? What were these situation ethics he talked about? How could he ever find out now, now that he had told that quick lie? Did they mean that, somehow, he felt himself to be above things like ordinary simple truth-telling? And if so, what did that imply about his attitude towards Sir Asif?

Sir Asif. Better hurry on up the stairs, or he would be waking up and coming out of his room and finding him with –

A sound, some small indefinable sound, at the head of the stairs came to his ears. He looked up.

Sir Asif was standing there looking down.

'Situation ethics, as I understand it, Doctor Ghote,' came that coldly articulate voice, 'means that what is considered the correct solution in any moral problem depends, not on general principles, but on the circumstances of that situation themselves. It is, if you like, the theory by which a man asks himself at every fresh instant, "Should I do to death this individual by whom I am confronted?" '

He felt yet more confused than ever, as if his mind was that expanse of roadway back in Bombay at Bori Bunder, where under the looming bulk of Victoria Terminus station at the peak of the morning rush, conflicting parties push themselves ruthlessly in every direction, cars twisting and turning and sharply hooting, long narrow pushcarts making their way past quickly as their straining coolies can stride, bicycles by the hundred, each with bell furiously ringing as if that and not its pedals was its motive-power, horse-drawn victorias pressing forward, cumbersome and slow, and thousands and thousands of walking office staff, of every kind and variety, hurrying this way and that, each one of them apparently dangerously late for work.

Was Sir Asif telling him, obliquely since he had refused to tell him anything directly, that the American priest was the person threatening him with death? Or had he just chosen that particular example out of the blue? Or had he chosen it with the deliberate purpose of putting confusion into the head of this irritatingly ever-present Doctor of Philosophy, as if he were a junior pleader who had had the temerity to waste the time of his court with some nonsensical argument?

He shook himself, as well as he could with the dragging weight of his suitcase still tugging at his extended arm.

'Thank you, sir,' he said. 'You have made that matter altogether clear.'

'Not at all, my dear fellow. I am, as you know, much in your debt. If I have in any way repaid it, I am more than pleased.'

Could he somehow swing the case behind his knees? Or was it too late for that?

'But, my dear Doctor, it is by no means yet time for tea, so I think I shall retire to my bed again. And I would advise you to take your case along to your room and do the same.

It's really extremely hot this afternoon.'

And the old man turned and slowly, but never shufflingly, made his way along the passage out of sight.

Below, he waited until he was sure that the Judge's bedroom door would be safely closed behind him and then, bending a little at the knees, he resumed his climb up the stairs. Once in his own room he let the weighty, excruciatingly coloured case drop and flopped down on to the bed.

Above him the fan was still managing to complete its every circuit. And still sounding as if, with each one, it was going to come at last to a stop. Errr-bock. Errr-bock. Errr-bock.

He thought about his released burden.

How absurd it had been of him to have had those ideas about what Sir Asif would feel if he saw it. It was a notion he had built up entirely in his own mind. Of course the old man was aware that not twenty-four hours earlier he had ordered him out of the house. Nothing that happened to remind him of that was going to alter his attitude to him now. By sheer good fortune it had fallen to him to do the old man a service, a great service, and that was not going to be forgotten just at the sight of a suitcase, however tan-coloured, however cardboardy.

No, for some obscure interior reason, he had erected a whole wall of fears and shames over the wretched object. He need never have toiled out in the sun to fetch it. All that had been a daytime nightmare he had blown up for himself. And in fact it had been another piece of good luck that Sir Asif had been disturbed by his conversation with Father Adam and had come out of his room and seen the disgraceful thing: that had shown him what a fool he had made himself. Absolutely unnecessarily.

He gave a long sigh.

A little self-knowledge was something. But it would not help him by one inch to solve the mystery of who had been typing there downstairs, of who it was who had put the other threatening notes in Sir Asif's way, of whether they truly meant to kill him on the anniversary of the Madurai sentences.

But the regular, rhythmical errr-bock, errr-bock of the fan above him soon took its toll. He fell asleep.

CHAPTER XVII

COMING ABRUPTLY awake, Ghote knew immediately, without any need to peer blearily at his watch, that he was late for tea. Cursing, he slid rapidly off the high bed, hurried across to the long mirror in the front of the dark carved almirah and did his best to make his crumpled clothes look presentable. No tie. Still down somewhere being ironed. It would be another black mark when he faced Sir Asif.

He pulled himself up.

What nonsense. Here he was already creating yet another burden for himself, erecting another barrier. Sir Asif would know very well why he had no tie and he would think none the worse of him for appearing at the tea-table without one. And he would think too, doubtless, that a guest who had started a long day with that fearful struggle with his mad son was entitled to sleep long in the afternoon.

No, he must not set up these walls in his mind. They were only a kind of excuse. Ways of making out that he was prevented from facing Sir Asif on equal terms. Because that was the heart of it. He was afraid of the man. Upside-down though it seemed, the fact of the matter always had been that it was the Judge, the possible victim, who was actually his opponent. So from the very beginning he had been scared, and had kept pretending that this opponent had special unfair advantages or that he himself had special disadvantages. Like the suitcase. He had done it so that he could avoid admitting that, when it came down to it, what he had to do was to stand up to the Judge and fight him, blow for blow. Psychological swipe for psychological swipe.

He felt suddenly pleased with that last phrase, and he had been thinking in English too. Psychological swipes. That might not be the language of one of Justice Asif Ibrahim's given judgements, but it had a strength of its own. He was getting better.

He took a last quick look in the mirror. Passable. He crossed over to the door, switched off the fan – it began a long dying whine the moment the hollow click of the switch had sounded – and left. To go down to tea.

They were seated on the wide terrace with its pillar-supported, shade-giving roof, Sir Asif, Begum Roshan with Mr Dhebar next to her, Father Adam and the Saint, in exactly the same positions as they had been the day before. On the brass tray with its spindly-legged stand there rested precisely the same plates as had been there before, in just the same places. Cucumber sandwiches, curry puffs and the small round cakes with their flat blobs of pink icing, soft in the heat. Did nothing ever change in the house? Would Sir Asif stay just as he was till the end, till his dying breath, an immovable opponent?

Psychological swipes, psychological swipes, he repeated to himself as he offered an apology for his tardiness.

But one thing had changed. Although he himself was late, Sir Asif had not ordered Raman to refrain from serving, as he had done when, out finding mad Sikander in his prison under the fort, he had been late for 'Drinks Before Dinner'.

No, the Doctor of Philosophy who had saved Raman from a terrible mauling this morning in the gardens was a different person in the Judge's eyes from the Doctor of Philosophy who had been imposed on him against his better judgement. So the obdurate old man could change his mind. On rare occasions.

He lowered himself on to the long, leaning cane chair that had been left for him. Raman came up with first tea that Begum Roshan had poured and then the plates of cucumber sandwiches and curry puffs.

Without hesitation he took one of the curry puffs he liked.

'I am glad you have joined us, Doctor Ghote,' Sir Asif said. 'I have been under attack, you know. Father Adam here has been arraigning me in the matter of capital punishment. I hope I may find an ally in you, my dear fellow.'

Capital punishment, he thought. The Madurai sentences. Was Father Adam delivering the next warning not as a typewritten note but as a veiled verbal threat? Perhaps because he had been disturbed before finishing typing what he had wanted to say?

'Oh, sir,' he answered Sir Asif, 'I am very much thinking you are altogether capable of defending yourself.'

'Perhaps I may be, perhaps I may be,' the Judge replied. 'Yet I frequently had occasion when I was on the Bench to warn litigants against presenting their own cases. It was very much a habit with political offenders, you know. Indeed, it happened in the Madurai Case, of which you may have heard. Though I am happy to say that there the defendants eventually took my advice and secured proper representation.'

The old devil, he thought. To name the case out loud, just like that. But it was typical of him. Typical. The unrepentant old devil.

Or, no, not unrepentant. Unyielding. That was it. Convinced that he had done right in those distant days, and nothing that he had found since having given him cause to alter his opinion.

But all the same a little wicked to tease that white Naxalite like that.

'Not that you, Judge, took much account of the arguments for the defence in that trial.'

The white Naxalite had risen to the bait like an obedient fish in a garden pool.

The Judge looked at him, back squarely upright in his high-backed peacock cane-chair, white pagri stiffly starched unmoving in the sluggish air, old veined hands grasping firmly the silver knob of his ebony stick.

'Now why should you believe I did that, Father?' he

asked. 'What evidence can you have for such an assertion about a case that was tried, surely, before you were even born?'

'A guy doesn't have to be there to know the facts.'

'No. No, indeed. But let me put it to you that he does have to have some evidence, some reliable evidence. Have you got that?'

'I've read enough about the case.'

'Ah, yes. And I dare say I could name the book you consulted. A number of curiously biased semi-histories about those days were written shortly after India attained independence. One of them at least deals with the Madurai Case at some length.'

'Well, maybe I did find out what I know about it from just such a book as you mention. Maybe the very one you have in mind. But that doesn't alter the facts. You were determined to find those men guilty from the very start, and you were determined they were going to be hanged at the end.'

Across the tea-table, where Raman had replaced the plates of cucumber sandwiches and curry puffs in exactly the same places as before, hot fury rolled in the hot stillness of the day.

But Justice Sir Asif Ibrahim was not dismayed by that. His flattened-nose face had lost nothing of its carved-stone immobility.

'No, my dear Father Adam,' he said without raising at all his voice. 'At the start of every trial over which I presided I went to some lengths to make sure that my mind was entirely open. At the end of any trial I had conducted I passed whatever sentence was appropriate.'

'That I'll accept when I accept pigs fly. You judges are all the same. You're bred to believe that you know best. Bred to believe that the police know best. Oh yes, every once in a while, when some evidence is just too strong, you make a parade of letting some poor guy go free. But if you can, you act just on behalf of society, or what you think of as society, which is nothing else than repression, repression of the have-nots in favour of the haves.'

Still the Judge was impassive in face of the tirade.

A silent spectator, he found himself wishing earnestly that he had slept and slept and never seen the cucumber sandwiches, the curry puffs and the little cakes with their slowly melting pink icing.

'No, there, Father, you are wrong. We judges are not all the same. I wish we were. I think we ought to be. But we are human beings and perfect judicial behaviour at all times is too much for us. There are judges, I grant, who like nothing better than to study the papers before a case comes to court and then to badger counsel throughout with their knowledge of the matter. And, yes, of them it can be said that they have made up their minds beforehand, and only the strongest evidence will shake them. But, and I ask you to believe this, the Indian Benches are singularly free of such men and have long been so.'

'And I don't believe it. Okay, maybe you genuinely do. You've been brought up to believe such things, believe against what you daily see and hear. You're blinkered, Judge. Blinkered over the justice of your courts, blinkered even over your own motives when you sent men daily to their deaths.'

'I think not.'

The Judge fell silent. But the force with which he had made his disclaimer was such that even the American priest plainly had no thought of producing any new barrage of assertions.

Then, after the silence had lengthened and lengthened and once Begum Roshan had jerked sharply forward as if she was about to throw in a comment of her own, only immediately to think better of it, Sir Asif spoke again.

'Yes,' he said, 'there is a case in point which I think at this distance of time there can be no grave harm in telling you of. You say that we judges cheerfully send men to their deaths. But let me tell you about someone who did precisely that, a quondam colleague of mine, or, to be accurate, a magistrate acting in a judicial capacity whom I once knew. A man who cheerfully sent other men to their deaths.'

The Saint, cross-legged on his low-slung cane chair, suddenly leant forward, much as Begum Roshan had done.

For an instant he expected to hear him speak.

But it was not urgent words that he interjected. It was a look. Nor was that his sun-beaming, radiantly reassuring smile. It was instead, plainly, a plea.

A plea, he guessed, more for Sir Asif to spare himself the telling of the reminiscence he was about to give them than for that reminiscence not to be heard at all. He shook his head. Surely he was being fanciful. You could not read that much into a mere look. Or could you?

But the Judge had turned his impassive face and was gazing out now at the parched colourless expanse of the gardens.

'I see no reason,' he said, 'even as a measure of abundant caution to withhold the man's name. He has been dead these many years. I read his obituary in the *Times of India*, and little enough that said.'

'Father – ' Begum Roshan broke in.

The Judge turned to her in an instant. 'When I need your comments, Roshan, I shall ask for them.'

And he left a silence then, long enough to allow his daughter to have her say and more, if she dared. She did not.

'He was called Farqharson-Wetherby. He was for a good many years a magistrate and he later became a judge, a Civil Service appointment, not a legal one. He was what they call an old *koi-hai*, which was not a bad description in his case. He spoke Tamil, of course, but in the club or the Bar common-room he never uttered more words in any Indian language than those. *Koi hai?* Who's there? And as soon as a bearer had presented himself, it was an order for whisky. And when he was not there in the common-room they used to talk about him.'

The Judge's old, articulate voice came to a halt, and once more the Saint directed at him that look of intense pleading.

And this time he was certain that it was saying, 'Spare yourself.'

But the Judge's gaze was fixed on the arid stretches of the gardens again. 'And the tale they most often told of Farqharson-Wetherby was of what he used to do when he came away from a hanging.'

Now Sir Asif turned and looked at them all.

'You know,' he asked, 'that it was the duty of a magistrate to attend hangings at any gaol within his district? It is a duty I myself in my young days fulfilled on a good many occasions. A magistrate has to be present. Well, these affairs always take place at exactly eight o'clock in the morning. It is the hour laid down. And depending on how far away one is from the gaol, one rises perhaps rather earlier than usual, one breakfasts, one sets off – '

'And you ate a good breakfast? You did?' Father Adam's tangled eyebrows were locked together more fiercely than ever.

Sir Asif sighed. 'Certainly on the first such occasion I had to attend I found difficulty in swallowing even so much as a cup of coffee,' he said. 'But later I found I was able to eat much my usual repast.'

It seemed that Father Adam was not going to intervene again.

'One arrives at the gaol,' Sir Asif resumed. 'The Superintendent is there to meet one. Generally in one's anxiety not to be late one has arrived in unduly good time. So the Superintendent shows you over his domain. Usually they are particularly proud of the gaol garden, and invariably they have long ceased to notice the pervasive smell which hangs over even that comparatively salubrious area, an odour of strong disinfectant combined with that of uncooked chapattis, since there is a regulation weight for the prison chapatti which is most easily attained by exposing them to the heat for less than the proper time.'

With a little moment of shock, he recognized the odour the Judge had described from the occasions he had had to visit prisons himself. The old man had hit on it exactly.

'Eventually one is taken to the appropriate condemned cell. One sees the prisoner, often just as he finishes that last meal for which by tradition he can have whatever he requests.' A long sigh. 'It is often a dish of curds.'

Nobody asked why.

'One then accompanies the wretched fellow to the place of execution. Sometimes he is resigned, sometimes he is in such a state of abject fear that a sedative of some sort has to be administered. Sometimes a fellow will defiantly sing. But that walk comes to an end for all of them and the hangman carefully places the fellow with one foot on either side of the broad slit that runs down the middle of the trap platform. He is given the opportunity to commend himself to his god. And then a black bag is placed over his head and over that the rope, adjusted so that its knot comes exactly under the angle of the left jaw to ensure the quick snapping of the jugular vein. Then all is ready. But it often happens that the exact hour of eight ack emma has not quite been reached. There may be three, four or even five minutes still to go. And the hangman does not pull his lever until the magistrate gives the signal.'

Again the Judge paused. The listening circle seemed as intent as if they themselves were that mandatory group of onlookers witnessing the execution.

'It was naturally my own invariable custom at once to give that signal,' Sir Asif resumed. 'On the very first occasion that I was faced with this situation I remember that some thoughts did cross my mind as to whether a last-minute reprieve might arrive, as in the story books. But I dismissed that then as fantasy, and nor did I allow it ever to affect me on any subsequent occasion. One cannot keep a fellow human waiting confined within that thick black bag for five whole minutes before he dies. However . . .' He looked directly at Father Adam. 'However, enforcing such delay was always the custom of Farqharson-Wetherby. And he boasted of it. It was said of him, too, that he seldom left a

gaol in these circumstances without humming that air of
Sullivan's to which William Schwenk Gilbert wrote the
words, "I heard one day a gentleman say that criminals who
are cut in two can hardly feel the fatal steel and so are slain
without much pain." Well, I will pass no strictures on him
for that. The mind plays curious tricks upon us. But what
I cannot forgive him is those three minutes, those four
minutes, those five. That man enjoyed inflicting torment.
He was not fit to occupy a judicial position.'

His stone face regarded the American priest unwaveringly.

'But, note,' he added, 'and this is my point: Farqharson-
Wetherby was cordially disliked by every single one of his
brothers on the Bench.'

Father Adam bit his lower lip. 'Well, I don't have to
accept that he was the only one,' he said.

Sir Asif gave a sharp little grunt. 'I hardly hoped that I
would convince you. But I thought it worth reviving the
memory of the man. He was, indeed, once quite abominably
rude to me in that same Bar common-room, to the point
of my deciding I had to refrain from using the place while he
was still there. But to me he is a singular example of the
man who takes up the shield of duty only to exercise a
personal power over other human beings, and I felt it
proper to put him before you in evidence.'

'Sir, you were right.'

He had not meant to speak.

He knew that it was not for him, a guest in the house, to
intervene in what was something not far short of an open
quarrel between his host and another guest. But listening to
Sir Asif's account of those prison scenes, seeing them
vividly as the old Judge had spoken, he had been carried
right away. And when the point Sir Asif had been making,
at such evident cost to himself, had been so unconsideringly
rejected, something in him over which he had no control had
broken out.

The Judge had shown himself, without intending it he
felt sure, to be a man who had never in fact let duty become

for him a garment of stiff hide under which he could let loose whatever strains of cruelty there were in his nature. He had shown himself to be a man who at every case had asked himself what his real duty was and then carried it out.

And in response he himself had been unable not to declare for him in whatever words first came.

But, appalled at the tactlessness he had heard issuing from his own lips, he sat now frozen. Awaiting retribution.

CHAPTER XVIII

THE JUDGE LOOKED at Ghote across the round brass tea-table and its plates of curry puffs, heat-curled cucumber sand-wiches and pink-iced cakes. The others too had their eyes fixed on him in the aftermath of his sudden, almost shouted declaration of support for Sir Asif, Begum Roshan as if she were on the point of bursting out with something herself, Mr Dhebar beside her as if he was slowly coming to a determination to ask this Doctor of Philosophy for a con-tribution to the controversial pages of *The Sputnik*, Father Adam as if yet another enemy of the socialist state had sprung up as might be expected, and the Saint with, once more, that smile, irradiating, penetrating, reassuring yet disturbing. Even Raman, who could not have understood more than a few words of the English conversation, seemed to be re-garding him as if he had in an instant taken on a whole new dimension.

It was the Judge who spoke first.

'Well, Doctor Ghote, I am relieved to have won your approbation, though of course I have hardly waited for that to feel secure in my own conscience.'

He felt the little sting in the words as if it was a stroke of the pliant twig with which the old schoolmaster of his earliest village days had taught the letters of the Nagari script. He was trying to frame some sort of apology for the outburst when the Judge spoke again.

'But I see that your tea-cup is empty, Doctor. Raman, what the devil have you been doing? Take the cup. Take it, take it, you fool. Take it to Begum Roshan. Hurry, hurry.'

Raman ducked at the Urdu onslaught upon him, grinned his horseshoe grin, wiped it off his face at once, grabbed at the cup and took it, chinking and clinking, over to Begum Roshan to be refilled.

He saw that when it came back he would have to drink it to the dregs, however stewed the tea might have got.

He saw something else too.

He saw what that outburst of his had really meant. It had been an immediate sign, immediate and unthinking, of a whole reversal that had taken place in his mind. He had come here to the old house warned of one thing: that he would find that the man he had been sent to protect was the biggest obstacle that he would face. He had been sent as a wedge, the Deputy Commissioner's wedge, to force himself quarter-inch by quarter-inch in towards the obstinate centre of that teak man and eventually to split him. He had, of course, failed. The Judge was of tougher wood than any brittle iron wedge up from Bombay could have forced apart. But he had at least pressed forward. The opposition had been there, and he had fought it.

But now, quite suddenly, with the Judge's account of that long-dead British magistrate, Farqharson-Wetherby, he had been shown the obdurate old man in a new light. It was, certainly, a light that had been there from the beginning, though he had not had eyes to see it. The plain fact of the matter was that the Judge was not the figure of sheer un-thinking obstinacy that he had thought him. He was, as his account of Farqharson-Wetherby had shown by contrast, a man who asked first what his duty was and only then carried it out. And did not cease from carrying it out while it was still to do.

So – Raman bent in front of him and deftly removed his plate with its few flaky crumbs of curry puff – the Judge's

conduct in face of the repeated threats made against his life
now looked altogether different. The man must have weighed
up the complete situation when that first note had mysteriously appeared at his side one day. He might even have come
to a definite conclusion about who its author was. He would
certainly have decided – it looked now – that the threat was a
perfectly serious one, that on the anniversary of the Madurai
sentences he would in all probability lose his life. And then
he must have come to the conclusion, taking into careful
account all the circumstances – 'all the evidence' he would
have said – that he was simply willing that his life should
come to an end. Life, he must have felt, now at his age held
little for him, and since he had been called on to sacrifice
it so as to re-assert for one final time his belief in the right-
ness of those sentences he had imposed at the end of the
Madurai Trial, sacrifice it he would. Cheerfully.

The tea-cup in his hand – the tea in it was fearfully
stewed – was less than half empty. He raised it to his
lips and swallowed.

So, if the Judge had not acted out of long-standing pre-
judice but had instead weighed with care the particular circumstances arising from these threats to his life and had
decided that he was willing to risk almost certain death –
Did that imply anything about the writer of the notes?
No matter just at this moment – then was not that a decision
which he, Inspector Ganesh Ghote, Bombay CID, Ganesh
Ghote, human being, was bound to respect? It was. It was.

And the consequences of that were clear too. It was now
his duty to go to the Judge and to tell him this. It was he
who had been the one with the inflexibly rigid view, not Sir
Asif, and he had been wrong. He had come to the old isolated
house with a fixed idea, that the Judge must be bullied or
tricked or somehow prevented from obstructing the protection that he ought to have and the investigation that was
necessary. But he should never have allowed himself to
have adopted that fixed notion. He should have asked
carefully what were the full circumstances and then have

acted in accordance with his findings.

Well, he would do that now.

But it would not be easy.

'Judge sahib,' he said, putting down his tea-cup which he saw now to be, thank goodness, almost empty. 'Judge sahib, I hope you will be able to spare me a few minutes before Drinks Before Dinner. There is something I have to tell you. Concerning the Memoirs, Judge sahib.'

The Judge looked at him. Stone face. Flattened nose. 'I had thought we had discussed every last point in the matter of the Memoirs, Doctor Ghote.'

'Sir, no. Sir, there is one fresh point which I feel I must bring to your attention.'

Stone face. Flattened nose. 'Very well, Doctor. Since you are so certain. Shall we say in about ten minutes' time?'

In the library those ten minutes later – dusk was coming rapidly down; it was already a little cooler; a servant was rolling up the pale brownish chick blinds outside the long windows to let in the maximum of evening air – the Judge looked as though he felt that once more he was dealing with a young and brash junior pleader, only this time he had him not in open court but in the privacy of his Chambers.

'Inspector, you have discussed this matter with me on several occasions already and taken up more time and more of an old man's fast-fading energies than I can easily spare. I thought I had made it clear that I have said everything on the subject that I wish to. Everything.'

'Sir, I have not come to ask. I have come to tell '

'Indeed, Inspector? Well, I trust that what you have to tell me is something I may hear with propriety.'

He did not know exactly.

He summoned up courage.

'Sir, it is this. I wish to withdraw from your house. I have come to see, sir, that you have every right not to have a police officer upon your premises if it is your considered desire not to do so. I had taken up an altogether wrong position, sir, I wish now to step back from that line.'

In the gathering gloom of the tall, book-looming room Sir Asif looked at him without speaking. Long slow seconds tocked out.

Then at last the old man spoke.

'I commend you, Inspector. It is not everyone who can resile from an untenable position which they have long held. But, please, do not feel obliged actually to leave. Stay here as my guest, my welcome guest. Your superiors, after all, would be glad to know that you were still here, I suppose.'

He thought of the Deputy Commissioner's strongly expressed unwillingness to release any of his officers for this remote and ungrateful task. He thought of the useful things he could do if he was back in Bombay. How much headway would they have made with the outbreak of foreign car stealing at places all over the city? And the Lokmanya Housing Society counterfeit gang, surely a few more days' observation there would produce a trail worth following up. No one else had had time for that, except himself.

But nevertheless the Deputy Commissioner would not, in fact, be pleased to see him before the day of the thirtieth anniversary of the Madurai sentences. And here in the house, well, if it turned out that he was actually there when the attempt was made on the Judge's life, he would do his best to prevent it. That might not be very logical, but life was not logical.

'Yes, sir,' he said. 'I would be honoured to stay.'

'Very well, my dear chap. That's settled. And there'll be no more nonsense about your fellow guests and my daughter?'

'No, sir. That is altogether finished now.'

So began for Ghote a strange period of time. His long battle with the Judge over, he found that the slow life of the household, which previously he had sharply resented, feeling it to be only another weapon of Sir Asif's in their struggle, seemed quite suddenly altogether satisfying. The meals, with their ceremonious prefaces and aftermaths, which had seemed so tediously unnecessary before, now fell into place marking the steady progress of the long, long days, occupying lengthy stretches of them, getting the time by in a fashion that was always more agreeable than not.

At the comparatively cool start of each day he would wait anxiously for chota hazri to be brought up to his room, that cup of tea and accompanying plantain which he would spend an extraordinarily long time in carefully consuming. And why not? Nothing awaited him. No longer were the stretched-out morning hours as the sun built up and up its deadening heat a good time in which to prowl the house hoping that he might, say, catch the Saint alone and find it was a day on which he was not vowed to silence.

The Saint, in fact, on the very first evening of this new period had taken his departure, as abruptly and casually as a dried-up fallen leaf might by the chanciest puff of air be whirled out of sight. From Raman next day Ghote had learnt that he was to address a huge meeting on the far side of the town followed by some others in the neighbourhood, but that he was expected, probably, to return. By then the news scarcely affected him: he was already too caught up in the meandering fish-tank life of the house.

After the few coolish hours of the early morning had passed there would come the late breakfast in the big dining-room. An English-style breakfast always, though with coffee in place of tea, but there would be fried eggs, toast, marmalade and, for the Judge at least, porridge.

Ghote had been offered that on his first morning in the house, but after a long cautious look at the grey glutinous stuff he had declined.

From its meal-marked start, each day would go slowly by to its meal-marked end, the long-drawn-out evening with first 'Drinks Before Dinner' and Sir Asif sipping his way through his two whisky-and-sodas while the rest of them sat making desultory conversation, and then dinner itself up on the wide flat roof in the heavy velvety night air with the large stars hanging in the dark blue sky over them and the candles in their deep-blue tall glasses on the long table almost burning as steadily. There would be more conver-

sation then, little spurts soon to be lost in the dry-sand river
bed of passing time. And now there would be excellent
food, Mughlai dishes with some taste to them in contrast to
the invariably awful luncheon, that dark brown, dull and
oily soup, the plain roast chicken, always scrawny, always
without any particular flavour, and after it the 'second toast',
the same three strips of salty tinned fish, dark on their same
small piece of flabby oil-soaked bread.

Occasionally Ghote found himself recalling the purpose of
his stay, the now overtaken purpose. He received a letter
from Headquarters in Bombay once, an answer both to his
deviously delivered inquiry about Mr Dhebar's past, of
which nothing was known, and to the telegram he had sent
from the railway station asking about Father Adam. Again
nothing to any purpose. Well, it mattered not. Nothing
mattered until that day came – it would not be long – when
it was the exact thirtieth anniversary of the ending of the
Madurai Trial when Sir Asif's life would be ended or
perhaps tranquilly continuing, the alarms of it all forgotten.

And then one day into the slow calm there came a sudden
small discordant sound. It was – he was surprised to have
realized – in fact the day before the anniversary of the
Madurai sentences. They were at tea, Sir Asif upright as
ever in his high-backed peacock chair, Father Adam lounging
as he always did, looking as ever the most unpriestlike of
priests, the Saint, who had, leaf-like, returned as unexpectedly as he had gone, cross-legged up on his chair,
eating nothing and, again, saying nothing, and Begum
Roshan presiding over the silver teapot.

And there had come then a scratching, loud and persistent.

He had turned to look. Any small disturbance in the slowly
turning day attracted disproportionate attention, not as a
relief from boredom, since now that he had accepted the
life it was no longer boring, but as something marking
pleasantly the passage of time.

It was one of the boy servants, a tousle-headed little

fellow dressed only in a pair of ragged khaki short pants,
half hiding behind the end pillar of the terrace. And the
scratching noise was made by his bare foot.

Raman hurried over to him, making shooing gestures. The
boy promptly disappeared round the corner. Raman followed him, reappeared a few seconds later and made his
way over to Sir Asif.

'Judge sahib, there is a person.'

'What person? Where? What on earth are you saying?
For heaven's sake try to make sense when you have occasion
to address me.'

'Yes, sir. Oh yes, sir. Sir, it is a person come with a
message.'

'A message? What message? Why hasn't whoever it is
been brought round here if it is a message for me?'

Was it another note? There had been none, so far as he
was aware, in the time since he had ceased to regard himself
as on duty. But this might be a new one. Though if so, it
was being delivered in a very public manner.

But in any case that was something for the Judge alone
now.

'Sir, it is not.'

'Not? Not what, man? Speak up, speak up. Don't stand
there like an idiot. What not, for heaven's sake?'

'Not for you, Judge sahib. Message for Doctor Ghote,
Judge sahib.'

Sir Asif darted a look of strong disapproval at him, and
he felt a flare of resentment – how could he have prevented this altogether unexpected interruption? – which
quickly died away. The merest ruffle on the day's calm
surface.

He got to his feet.

'Perhaps I had better go and see who it is.'

'Yes, yes. In the middle of tea.'

The Judge took a long drink from his cup as if this
enormous event might prevent him ever tasting tea again.

Round the corner of the house he found that the messenger

was a constable, carefully not wearing uniform, and that he
had brought a letter from the District Superintendent of
Police.

> I regret to have to inform you that a quantity of gelignite,
> intended for blasting operations on the bund at the extreme
> end of gardens of Sir Asif Ibrahim (operation postponed
> owing to legal action) has been misappropriated. Further
> regret to inform that said gelignite is reported to be in
> unstable condition.

For a moment as he read, the soft-wrapping time-haze
was whipped away by a quick unspringing typhoon wind
and his mind was instantly full of thoughts of actions and
consequences, of trains of logic, of ifs and ands. If gelignite
really had been stolen, had it been taken for the purpose of
killing Sir Asif? That death by explosion for the man who had
sentenced to death the explosives conspirators of Madurai?
And if that was so, then which of them seated round the
tea-table there was most likely to have been the thief or
arranged the theft? And did the fact of such a theft mean
that any one of them was automatically cleared?

But then the thought of that other teatime, not so many
days before, came back to him. Sir Asif had shown then that
he was no Farqharson-Wetherby, mind made up from
earliest youth. He had shown then that he had earned the
right to die in the way he had chosen.

So he stuffed the letter into his pocket, thanked the
constable and returned to the group on the terrace.

'Raman, Doctor Ghote's cup is empty. What in God's
name do you think you are here for, man? It is to look after
people's cups and see whether they need more tea. That is
your duty. Do you understand? Your duty.'

And Raman's shame-faced horseshoe smile coming and
going.

The incident began to seem no more than the most casual
of eddies on the slow stream of their daily life. Tea took its

course again. He ventured on a cake, although its icing under the heat had dripped to the very edge. And then the full significance of that letter erupted in his mind.

Said gelignite is reported to be in unstable condition.

The stuff was dangerous. Highly dangerous. And not just to its intended victim. Nor simply to whichever one of them it was who had got hold of it. It was dangerous to everybody in the whole of the old house.

CHAPTER XIX

GHOTE MADE HIMSELF wait until tea was over, until the last second cup had been drained, the last little cake with its sliding pink icing had been refused. And then when the Judge in his customary fashion had risen to his feet with the aid of his silver-topped stick and had begun to move slowly off to the library where he invariably spent the time after tea, he made his way over to him as soon as he was on his own, pulling from his pocket as he did so the warning message.

'Sir,' he said in a low voice, 'I think you also ought to see the communication I received.'

The Judge looked at him with a small frown of disapproval. 'Really, Doctor? I thought we had agreed that I need be no further consulted over those wretched – ahem – Memoirs.'

It took a small effort to continue confronting that stone visage. But he made it.

'Sir, I think you would find that the situation has changed. Please read this, sir.'

Sir Asif took the sheet of paper he had thrust out, coarse-textured and buff in colour, more than a little crumpled from having been crammed into his trouser pocket. He smoothed it out. He read.

'Unstable condition, sir. It means that it might explode on a slight impact only, or from a mere spark, or anything.'

The Judge said nothing, stood sombrely regarding the

creased sheet in his hand.

And at last answered. 'Very well. Be so good, then, as to accompany me to the library.'

Slowly they progressed through the dim-shaded, furniture-crowded drawing-room, down the long passage that led from it, into the entrance hall, wide and airy with the great carved staircase leading up from it, down the equally long passage that took them to the library and at last into that tall, book-lined room, the Judge's stick tap-tapping an irregular, maddening rhythm every step of the way.

And at every step he found himself back once more fiercely resenting the terribly slow pace of existence in the old house. Here now was something urgent. Something to be dealt with at once. Something calling for immediate questions and immediate answers. And the old man was insisting on installing himself in his customary fashion in the library before he would give the matter any attention at all.

And when he did bring his mind to it, what would he say? Would he realize that the situation had changed? That it was vital to find out who had got hold of the gelignite – he saw it in his mind's eye, yellowish muddy bars oozing an oily sweat – and to take it from them before some tiny chance split wide the whole old house in a roar of scarifying orange flame?

The Judge lowered himself into his customary chair.

Mind now alert and rapid-moving, he glanced immediately at the ivory-inlaid table beside it for yet another warning note. And there was one there. The familiar thick sheet of folded white paper tucked just under the base of the tall lamp, a sheet that could have been placed there with ease by anyone knowing the invariable routine of this routine-chained house. By any one of them.

'Excuse me, sir,' he said.

And he leant across the old man's thin fleshless legs under their unspotted white silk trousering and tweaked the folded sheet from its place.

'I expect this is for you, sir,' he said.

He made no attempt to unfold the note. The Judge glanced up at him and took it with a little grunt of acknowledgement.

He waited to see what the old man would do. If he were to read it and at once put it in his pocket as he had done before, or, worse, not to read it and to put it away, then he would know that he was still clinging to his obstinately held belief that the whole affair was an entirely private matter.

'Inspector, I think you should examine this with me. It may be helpful to you.'

'Yes, sir.'

The Judge unfolded the sheet.

I therefore sentence you.

'Well, Inspector,' the old man said, 'my communicant certainly practises a commendable economy of style.'

'Your communicant, sir?' he said. 'Does that mean that you have not already put a name to this person?'

Yet had he? Had he secretly done so? And was he now still determined not to reveal that secret?

'Alas, no, Inspector, I have not. Their identity is unknown to me completely. And, be sure, I would tell you if I knew it. The situation demands no less.'

'Yes, sir. And do you then wish me to make inquiries? Every inquiry that I can?'

'I do, Inspector. We cannot have innocent persons killed simply because some unknown is conducting a vendetta against myself.'

'No, sir. Of course not, sir. But, sir, would you still agree that the number of persons about whom I have to make inquiries is very much limited?'

'Oh yes, Inspector. Limited to typewriter-using individuals with access to this table.'

And the Judge's old veined fleshless hand reached out and tapped sharply once – a little dull thud – on the intricately ivory-decorated surface beside him.

'Yes, Inspector. Let me name them. My visitor, Father

Adam, priest of the Roman Catholic Church, citizen of the United States of America. My occasional visitor, Mr Dhebar, in whose minimally circulating journal I have chosen to publish my *obiter dicta*. My old friend, now turned into peripatetic holy man, the self-styled Anand Baba. And, not to neglect any possibility, my own daughter, despite her having insisted, wisely as it now proves, on your own presence here, my dear fellow.'

'Yes, sir. I do not see how the person I am looking for can be any other than those. With one possible addition, sir.'

He hesitated. And the Judge spoke before he had gone on.

'Ah, I see, Inspector, that you must be aware that Anand Baba visits my poor Sikander. And you suspect some sort of collaboration. Very well, add Sikander to your list.'

'Thank you, sir. And, sir . . .'

'Yes, Inspector?'

'Would you kindly tell me now everything that you know about each of these individuals? To help me in my – '

'Of course, Inspector. Could you believe otherwise?'

'No, sir. No, I could not.'

'Very well then. What is it exactly you wish to know?'

He thought rapidly. 'Well, sir, Shri Anand Baba. How is it that he comes to be here at all, sir? Is it true that he was utterly opposed to you at the time of the Madurai Conspiracy Case?'

'Yes, Inspector, that is perfectly true. Anand Baba, as he is now called, was in my young days a fellow student. And, let me say it, the only one amongst them who was my better. Yet we were friends, close friends despite our difference of religion. But later our ways divided. He took to politics. I cleaved to the law. He became indeed what is nowadays called a terrorist, and eventually took poor Sikander, then already nearly deranged, under his wing. So we were as opposed one to the other as it was possible to be. But then, when with the passing of the years Anand Baba abandoned violence and took to preaching, why, we became reconciled. He visits me now whenever he is nearby. For the pleasure of my company, I believe, and in an endeavour to make some amends for Sikander, whose final disintegration he feels some responsibility for.'

'I see, sir. And the matter of collaboration between them, do you find that likely?'

'No, Inspector, I do not. But then in my days on the Bench I was frequently faced with incontrovertible evidence of behaviour that no one would have called likely. The human being has an almost inexhaustible capacity for committing acts of unmitigated folly.'

'Yes, sir.'

He thought again. 'Sir, your daughter?'

'Ah, yes. Roshan. Did she insist on your presence here in order, so to speak, to disguise what she herself was doing? And will she, if that is so, continue to the point of parricide? I tell you, Inspector, I do not know. Many years ago I saw it as my duty to prevent her marrying a young Hindu. It seemed to me then that marriages across the religious boundary were fraught with potential disaster. I suppose that nowadays there have been enough such unions for people to have learnt a little how to conduct themselves in the difficult course they have embarked upon. Though I often doubt it. So I still believe that I was right to do what I did then for my motherless child. But even if she has not borne me all these years a grudge – and I am by no means sure that she has not – it is plain that her life has been deeply affected by her failure ever to marry. And so, yes, I suppose she might be capable of parricide. Or of anything.'

'Even, sir,' he said, conscious of great daring, 'of marrying Mr Dhebar?'

Sir Asif gave him a single quick look and then burst out into laughter. Soon tears were running down his ancient leathery cheeks, glistening at the sides of his curiously flattened nose.

'Sir. Sir. Please, sir.'

If the old man went on longer he would exhaust himself.

'I – I – Oh, excuse me, Inspector. I – I am sorry. But does

that – does that intolerable fool really nurture an idea of
that sort?'

'Yes, sir, he does. And, sir, I know very well what you are
meaning when you say "intolerable fool", but nevertheless,
sir, Mr Dhebar is a person of great determination.'

Sir Asif wiped the last tear from his chin. 'Yes, Inspector.
You're right, of course. A person of enormous determination.
How else with his abilities would he have reached even where
he has got to? So therefore, I grant you, a potential murderer.
Yes, you must look out for Dhebar, Inspector. Though I do
not think I shall ever have the pleasure of attending my
daughter's wedding to him, provided, that is, that we find
this dangerous stuff of yours.'

'Very well, sir. And that leaves only Father Mort Adam,
sir. He is here, isn't it, because your cousin at the Pakistan
Embassy in Washington asked you to look after him in his
illness, sir? But is there more to it than that? Sir, is he truly a
Roman Catholic priest?'

Sir Asif laughed again then. But it was no more than a
short and sharply contemptuous bark.

'Yes, Inspector. Extraordinary though it may seem to
you, and to myself, that man is a priest. As well, of course,
as a stick-at-nothing socialist, a fellow who has been in
trouble both in America, which was why he was sent to
India as some sort of medical assistant, and to some extent
with the authorities here. Oh yes, there's another one to
watch, Inspector.'

He felt a rapid sliding-down of depression at these last
words. They meant that between them they had come to the
end of their list of possibles. And somehow he had expected
that something which the Judge had been keeping secret
about one of the people on that list – but the old man had
not been keeping secrets, only not gossiping to a stranger –
would be a piece of hard information that would lead him
at last to the writer of those threatening notes. But there had
been nothing. Nothing.

And next day that still unreachable person would attempt

to put the stolen gelignite where it would kill Justice Sir
Asif Ibrahim 'by means of an explosive detonation'. And in
all probability in making the attempt would blow up more
than one innocent person in the house.

I therefore sentence you. He glanced down again at the
warning the Judge had just received where it rested open
on the ivory-inlaid table. Yes, its few words sounded the
note of finality well enough. He could almost hear Sir Asif, or,
no, another Judge, saying them in a hushed court as he
finished pronouncing a Guilty verdict. Those would be the
exact words.

The exact words.

Feverishly then he tried to recall with complete accuracy
the wording of the other two notes he had known about.
Of course, the one Begum Roshan had seen might have got
considerably distorted before it had come to him. But the
other one, the one he had read for himself here in this very
room before Sir Asif had put it in his pocket, that one he
could surely remember letter for letter.

*Judge. 12 days only remaining. May the Lord have mercy
upon your soul.*

Yes, that was it. And it was in just the same sort of wording
as the note there on the table now. Wording that could have
come from the very lips of a judge.

'Sir Asif,' he burst out, his voice rising with excitement.
'Sir Asif, can you confirm something for me? The language
of this note here, sir, it is the language of a judge passing a
sentence, isn't it?'

'Why, yes,' the old man said. 'Yes, it is.'

'And, sir, the other notes you have received, were they in
similar language also?'

Sir Asif thought for a little. 'Yes, Inspector, they were.
Each one of them. I had not realized it till this moment,
but they were. They might all have been written by a judge.'
The old man frowned. 'But, surely, Inspector, no judge
could possibly have left any of the notes here in this house?
We had agreed that the person responsible must be someone

with easy access to myself. I suppose that in a way Anand Baba might have – '

'No, sir, no,' he interrupted, swept away on the flowing tide of his logic. 'Sir, it is not a judge we are looking for. We have altogether drawn the line in the wrong place, sir. We have said that no one in the household was enough educated to use a typewriter except for those on our list, sir, and we have drawn the line underneath those names. But, sir, we were wrong. It is not too difficult just to press down the keys of a typewriter, not at all difficult. Not to use a typewriter to copy with only, sir. Anyone with a minimum of education could do that, with a minimum of English even. If they had the right words to follow. A judge's words, sir.'

He took a wild gulp of air.

'As a judge's orderly would have,' he said.

CHAPTER XX

BUT RAMAN, when Inspector Ghote hurried out to look for him, was nowhere to be found.

For hour after hour afterwards the Judge sat in his tall chair in the library, keeping his erect posture only with obvious effort, and directed every servant and gardener he could summon in a search of the whole of the house and the dark gardens. But from the first it was clear that Raman must somehow have got wind of the possibility that he had been discovered – Could he have been listening standing up against the house wall just outside the tall library windows? Had he found out from the police constable messenger that a warning about the stolen gelignite had been delivered? – and that he had taken good care to hide himself somewhere where it was very unlikely that he would be found. The gardens, with their tall growths of dried grasses, their little-tended old bushes, their once elegant sunken areas here and there, their tall ancient easily climbed trees, were made for hiding in. And the handful of gardeners and their boys, beset by fears of the ghosts said to haunt the old fort, were hardly the most diligent of searchers.

In between sending out fresh parties to new locations, and to old locations yet once more, Sir Asif listened with exhausted patience to Ghote's explanations.

'Sir, all along I ought to have seen it. Damn it, sir, I found him just outside this very room at the time you had been left the note saying, "Twelve days only remaining", and, sir, there was the fact of that "twelve" being written in figures only, that should have been a clue to me. And then when I heard someone typing in one of the rooms in the passage leading to the kitchen quarter I actually found him lying there in the kitchen, only I believed he was sleeping. Because I did not think of him at all, sir, as being possible. I had drawn that line, sir, under the typewriter-using individuals. That appalling line.'

'As I had, too, Inspector. As I had, too. It was a reasonable assumption to make. Perfectly reasonable.'

'Well, sir, I do not know. Certainly Raman seldom used any words of English, and when he did he got them altogether muddled.'

'Yes, there was every reason to put him out of account, my dear fellow. And I still do not understand why he should have chosen the thirtieth anniversary of my sentences in the Madurai Case as his *terminus ad quem*. What interest was that to him?'

Terminus ad quem was what he himself did not understand, though he could make a guess at what it meant. The final hour. For the Judge.

'Sir, I think it was like this,' he replied. 'Raman was not, as you said, particularly concerned about the Madurai Trial. He was concerned about his own trial shortly before that. When you freed him on the ground of – what was it, sir? – *falsus in uno, falsus in omnibus*. He thought always, you know, sir, that you had released him simply in order to be your Orderly. And you told him then that if you had had to sentence him you would have given him thirty years. So he got it into his head that he had to serve just thirty years in your employ.'

'Good God, man, you're perfectly right. The wretch tried to give me his notice just a few weeks ago, told me in so many words that he had served his thirty years and wanted to go home, to the South. I couldn't make out what the thirty years nonsense was all about, and I told him that in any case he would be a fool to give up a job in which he was perfectly happy. And he was happy, you know. He was. Of course, I slanged him from time to time, but he never took any notice of that.'

'Yes, sir, I agree. Whatever you said to him, sir, did not at all disturb him. He was a most extraordinarily patient fellow. Except for his one sticking-point, sir: that he thought that at the end of thirty years he would be allowed to go home, to a home, I expect, that he believed would be just as it had been thirty years ago.'

'Yes, he certainly believed that. Told me as much on many occasions. And nothing I could say would persuade him that it would not be so.' The Judge sighed deeply. 'But none of this alters the fact that the fellow has got hold of this danger-ous explosive of yours, Inspector. And that must be found. If we have to stay up all night to find it, we must get hold of it before it kills someone else.'

And they did stay up all night. But they did not find the gelignite. And they did not find Raman.

But they found his traces.

It was at a very late stage of the night. The big old house was still busy. Servants carrying lanterns were hurrying here and there, quite pointlessly for the most part. Lights in the rooms where they were installed were being flicked on and off. And then, for no particular reason, it came into Ghote's head where Raman would have hidden his stolen explosive.

He had left the library then without a word to Sir Asif, had run all the way up the wide stairs, had hurried fast as he could to the long-deserted bedroom that Sir Asif had once shared with Lady Ibrahim. Without ceremony he had burst in, run round to where on the far side of the big high bed with its stiffly folded bedcover there was that pile of light wooden crates containing the objects ordered from distant Bombay by Lady Ibrahim before she had died and scarcely opened on their arrival.

He had carefully lifted the thin wooden lid of the top crate. And had found what he had guessed would be there.

Or nearly so. Because there was not the half-dozen oozing sticks of explosive he had hoped for nestling among the wood shavings that had for so many years protected a once latest-fashion table lamp, only the wrapper from one of them, stained and unmistakable, and a faint whiff of a rich, mechanical, unpleasant odour.

'Well, sir,' he said when he reported his discovery to Sir Asif, 'it means one thing for certain. He is definitely somewhere near, waiting for his chance to use the stuff.'

'Yes, my dear chap, I think we must accept that conclusively now. But you know this house. He could hide in it for a week and evade capture.'

'Yes, sir.' He looked, with eyes suddenly stiff with tiredness, at his watch. 'Well, sir, it must be getting on for first light now. We can expect something at any time.'

'I dare say the fellow will wait until it is fully light,' Sir Asif said. 'Official time means little to him. As far as he's concerned a day begins with the daylight.'

'Yes, sir.'

'So, Inspector, as soon as the day does begin, I wish to be left alone in here. Quite alone. Is that understood?'

He understood at once. The old man saw it as his duty to isolate himself completely, so that if Raman did succeed in setting off the gelignite where and when he intended it would kill no one but himself.

It was a brave decision.

But, he realized, he would have been disappointed if the Judge had said anything else.

'Yes, sir. I do understand.'

'Good.'

The old man looked up at him then. 'But, Inspector.'

'Yes, sir?'

'Find him if you can. Find him and tell the foolish fellow that if he wants to go and live in the South, well, of course he can go. And that when he realizes things are not quite as he had expected them, I'll have him back.'

'Yes, sir.'

He went then to try to get some more order into the bleating chaos of the search. But he knew that if they did hit on Raman's hiding-place it would be no more than by luck. The house was too big. It was too old. It had too many never-visited nooks and crannies. A search for signs of occupation in one of its many rooms, like his own in the early days of the affair, was a reasonably practical proposition. If someone had been living in some particular part of the house, it had been reasonable to hope to find signs of that. But to dig out anyone playing hide-and-seek amid all its many possibilities was quite another matter.

And there were the gardens, too.

So when at last the night, such a night as the old house had not known for years, perhaps for a century, came to an end, nothing more had been discovered. The traceried windows showed the first thin white light of the new day. From across the river came the frenzied sound of the milkman's muzzled calf as he drove his cow up to the kitchen quarter. And the situation was just as it had been when they had first realized that Raman had gone missing.

He went down to see Sir Asif again. The old man was sitting in his chair where he had been almost all the night. His eyes looked as if they were closed.

He coughed.

The Judge jerked more upright. 'Ah. Ah, it's you, my dear chap. And daylight. Daylight, too. Would you be good enough to put out that lamp? And then if you'll leave me.'

'Yes, sir. Yes. But . . .'

'But what, my dear fellow?'

'But, sir, is there nothing that I can do for you?'

'No, no. Just make sure no idiot of a servant comes trying to bring me anything. I shan't need it, whatever it is.'

The deep-sunk eyes in the leathery face on either side of that squashed-flat nose looked at him with a sudden sharp twinkle.

'I dare say I shall never need anything any more.'

'Well, sir, I hope we can catch him before he gets to you.'

'Before he sets that damned stuff off by accident and kills someone else, Inspector.'

'Yes, sir.'

He left him for the last time then. There was nothing else to do.

And the slow morning went slowly by. He superintended a new and better search of the gardens. He even took it on himself to carry Sikander's tray out to the fort, nurturing a tiny hope that his own hunt there the night before had not been thorough enough. But it was a vain hope.

He prowled round the area of the house which he had ordered to be evacuated, hoping somehow to intercept Raman on his way with the gelignite. But he knew that it was not practical to prevent every access, and he was not sure that he altogether wanted to. If Raman could be attracted by Sir Asif sitting alone there in the library and came out into the open, perhaps that would be the best way of dealing with the situation.

The cook produced breakfast, as always. There was porridge for Sir Asif that stood all the while cooling in his empty place. But no one ate very much of anything.

And lunch, too, appeared as usual. The same oily brown soup, the same scrawny roasted chicken. Begum Roshan wanted to take a tray to her father. But he managed to persuade her that the gesture would not be appreciated.

But, just as the meal was over, the old man emerged himself from his seclusion.

'I am going upstairs to sleep,' he said. 'Someone as old as I am needs his rest, and I cannot get mine in that chair there. So, Ghote, my good fellow, will you see that no one goes anywhere near my room?'

'Yes, of course, Sir Asif. And, sir, since he has made no attempt up to now, do you think that after all he means not to? That he has changed his mind, sir?'

'No,' the Judge answered, his voice level and elaborately articulate as ever. 'No, I think that he still intends to murder me. I am, you know, the man who did not release him at the end of his thirty-year term for another murder.'

He watched him turn and leave. Slow steps, but steady ones, cane tap-tapping in front of him.

He felt a gush of admiration for the man. To face his end like that, with so much calm. To see his duty and simply to do it. He imagined him, after he had made his way step by step up the stairs, going slowly into his room, the room he had occupied for so many years, and there taking his afternoon sleep as in the ever-repeated way of the old house it was his custom to do. His bed would be awaiting him, if for once without its cover turned down by his Orderly of thirty years. And neither would the fan above the bed have been switched on. Did that one too go maddeningly 'errr-bock, errr-bock' all afternoon? Probably it did. From what he had seen of it when he had gone into the room during his search of the house all those days ago, it had been –

The thought came to his mind like a hammer-blow.

In an instant he had pelted along the passage in the Judge's wake. Not in the hall. Not on the stairs. He tore up those in his turn, straining leg muscles, arms extended in front of him.

He reached the stairhead. He flung himself round.

Not there. Not in the passage.

But the door of his room was still open, a flood of white light pouring into the shadowy passage.

'Stop,' he shouted.

He ran forward, slithered on the veiny marble of the floor, reached the doorway.

The Judge was standing there, leaning on his stick. His hand was reaching out to the bakelite switch for the fan.

He dived forward, arm thrust out. He knocked the frail, high-veined hand down just one moment before it would have flicked on the switch.

And, sure enough, after many apologies and explanations, when he clambered up on to the Judge's high, hard bed, without even removing his shoes, and peered at the un-turning fan hanging there, it was quite plain that the bowl-shaped motor-casing had recently been removed and re-placed. The gap between its upper rim and the cracked plaster of the ceiling was a good deal wider than it had been and, just visible in it, there was a corner of greasily stained paper like the piece he had found in the crate in Lady Ibrahim's long-preserved room next door.

'Yes,' he said to the Judge, backing half a step on the hard cushiony surface of the bed. 'Yes, it is here. We have found it. All is well.'

He saw Sir Asif's flattened-nose face peer up at him, marked by a clear anxiety.

'My dear fellow, that is excellent. Excellent. But you aren't going to attempt to remove the stuff, are you?'

Ghote looked down at him. 'Oh no, sir,' he answered. 'No, no. There are some things where I altogether draw the line.'

Steve Knickmayer

CRANMER

Something is rotten in the town of Two Kettle. It's a small town with a big secret. And when Cranmer arrives to find his friend's body being dragged from the river, he soon suspects that nobody can be trusted.

Maneri – The easy-going private investigator seems friendly. But is he harbouring a murderous grudge?

Brenda – Maneri's sister is desired by many men . . . a beautiful woman until someone smashes up her face.

Satterfield – The bank clerk vanishes after the murder – and becomes the prime suspect.

Cohen – The Police chief blames Cranmer for bringing a crime wave into the town.

O'Hearn – He was the victim . . . but what is the secret that remains hidden in his wallet?

Cranmer is going to find out – even if it kills him!

'Fast paced, violent, sexy' – *Publishers Weekly*

UK 90p   0 600 32046 4

James Patterson

THE JERICHO COMMANDMENT

One of the most shocking novels of revenge you will ever read THE JERICHO COMMANDMENT

A ghastly secret born in the Nazi extermination camps now rises again to corrupt the living. And the innocent as well as the guilty are sucked into its horrendous vortex.

– A mysterious terror group so hungry for vengeance that justice is distorted into madness.

– An 80-year-old millionairess whose defection from 'the Cause' provokes a series of murders that panic America.

– Successful young doctor, David Strauss, driven by the massacre of his family into desperately following the 35-year-old trail of phantom Nazis.

– Beautiful Alix Rothschild, survivor of Dachau, now America's leading fashion model yet somehow part of the deadly scheme.

– The FBI gradually hunting down the killers and discovering a plot more horrible than even they could have fantasized . . .

With an ultimatum delivered at the 1980 Olympic Games in Moscow this heritage of malignant passions is finally brought to a gruelling climax.

'The Jericho Commandment is a stick-to-your-chair thriller that will give a large body of readers galloping nightmares' – Thomas N. Scortia, author of *The Glass Inferno*

UK £1.00   0 600 35273 0

Gregory Mcdonald

FLYNN

A moonlight night – a sudden explosion – and burning people fall out of the sky.

Flynn is a highly unusual cop – smart and tough, but witty and gentle too – and he now has 118 murders to solve.

When the Boeing 707 explodes – and Flynn sees it drop into Boston harbour from his front window – he is called in to investigate.

Was it political sabotage (an Arab minister was on board), or mass murder (the Human Surplus League are pledged to solve over-population by wholesale slaughter), or just plain murder? There is no shortage of suspects: the judge with the new young wife who has taken out a huge life-insurance policy ... the great English actor who has just stormed out of the first night of *Hamlet* ... the young boxing champion with underworld connections ...

It takes all Flynn's wit and brilliance to uncover the surprise solution. And he does it in a manner as stylish and outrageous as would do credit to his friend Fletch.

'Witty, intriguing and superb entertainment' – *Yorkshire Post*

'Flynn is one of the smartest, gentlest, most sarcastic cops you will ever meet' – *The New York Times*

UK 95p   0 600 33675 1

FICTION

CRIME/ADVENTURE/SUSPENSE

☐ The Organization	David Anthony	90p
☐ Stud Game	David Anthony	95p
☐ Five Pieces of Jade	John Ball	85p
☐ Siege	Peter Cave	£1.15
☐ The Execution	Oliver Crawford	90p
☐ The Ransom Commando	James Grant	95p
☐ The Rose Medallion	James Grant	90p
☐ Barracuda	Irving A. Greenfield	95p
☐ The Halo Jump	Alistair Hamilton	£1.00
☐ The Desperate Hours	Joseph Hayes	95p
☐ A Game for the Living	Patricia Highsmith	95p
☐ The Blunderer	Patricia Highsmith	95p
☐ Those Who Walk Away	Patricia Highsmith	95p
☐ The Tremor of Forgery	Patricia Highsmith	80p
☐ The Two Faces of January	Patricia Highsmith	95p
☐ The Heir	Christopher Keane	£1.00
☐ Cranmer	Steve Knickmeyer	90p
☐ The Golden Grin	Colin Lewis	£1.00
☐ Confess, Fletch	Gregory Mcdonald	90p
☐ Fletch	Gregory Mcdonald	90p
☐ Flynn	Gregory Mcdonald	95p
☐ To Kill a Jogger	Jon Messmann	95p
☐ Pandora Man	Kerry Newcomb and Frank Schaefer	£1.25
☐ Sigmet Active	Thomas Page	£1.10
☐ The Jericho Commandment	James Patterson	£1.00
☐ Games	Bill Pronzini	85p
☐ Crash Landing	Mark Regan	95p
☐ The Mole	Dan Sherman	95p
☐ Swann	Dan Sherman	£1.00
☐ The Peking Pay-Off	Ian Stewart	90p
☐ The Seizing of Singapore	Ian Stewart	£1.00
☐ Place of the Dawn	Gordon Taylor	90p
☐ Judas Cross	Jeffrey M. Wallmann	90p
☐ Rough Deal	Walter Winward	85p
☐ The Ten-Tola Bars	Burton Wohl	90p

HISTORICAL ROMANCE/ROMANCE/SAGA

☐ Flowers of Fire	Stephanie Blake	£1.00
☐ So Wicked My Desire	Stephanie Blake	£1.50
☐ Morgana	Marie Buchanan	£1.35
☐ The Enchanted Land	Jude Deveraux	£1.50
☐ Mystic Rose	Patricia Gallagher	£1.25
☐ Alinor	Roberta Gellis	£1.20
☐ Gilliane	Roberta Gellis	£1.00
☐ Joanna	Roberta Gellis	£1.25
☐ Roselynde	Roberta Gellis	£1.20
☐ Love's Scarlet Banner	Fiona Harrowe	£1.00
☐ Lily of the Sun	Sandra Heath	95p
☐ Daneclere	Pamela Hill	£1.25
☐ Strangers' Forest	Pamela Hill	£1.00
☐ Royal Mistress	Patricia Campbell Horton	£1.50
☐ The Tall One	Barbara Jefferis	£1.00
☐ Captive Bride	Johanna Lindsey	£1.00
☐ The Flight of the Dove	Catherine MacArthur	95p
☐ The Far Side of Destiny	Dore Mullen	£1.50
☐ The Southern Moon	Jane Parkhurst	£1.25
☐ Summerblood	Anne Rudeen	£1.25
☐ The Year Growing Ancient	Irene Hunter Steiner	£1.10

HAMLYN WHODUNNITS

☐ The Worm of Death	Nicholas Blake	95p
☐ The Judas Pair	Jonathan Gash	95p
☐ There Came Both Mist and Snow	Michael Innes	95p
☐ The Siamese Twin Mystery	Ellery Queen	95p

FICTION

GENERAL

- Stand on It — Stroker Ace — 95p
- Chains — Justin Adams — £1.25
- The Master Mechanic — I. G. Broat — £1.50
- Wyndward Passion — Norman Daniels — £1.35
- Abingdon's — Michael French — £1.25
- The Moviola Man — Bill and Colleen Mahan — £1.25
- Running Scared — Gregory Mcdonald — 85p
- Gossip — Marc Olden — £1.25
- The Sounds of Silence — Judith Richards — £1.00
- Summer Lightning — Judith Richards — £1.00
- The Hamptons — Charles Rigdon — £1.35
- The Affair of Nina B. — Simmel — 95p
- The Berlin Connection — Simmel — £1.50
- The Cain Conspiracy — Simmel — £1.20
- Double Agent—Triple Cross — Simmel — £1.35
- Celestial Navigation — Anne Tyler — £1.00
- Earthly Possessions — Anne Tyler — 95p
- Searching for Caleb — Anne Tyler — £1.00

WESTERN   BLADE SERIES

- No. 1   The Indian Incident — Matt Chisholm — 75p
- No. 2   The Tucson Conspiracy — Matt Chisholm — 75p
- No. 3   The Laredo Assignment — Matt Chisholm — 75p
- No. 4   The Pecos Manhunt — Matt Chisholm — 75p
- No. 5   The Colorado Virgins — Matt Chisholm — 85p
- No. 6   The Mexican Proposition — Matt Chisholm — 75p
- No. 7   The Arizona Climax — Matt Chisholm — 85p
- No. 8   The Nevada Mustang — Matt Chisholm — 85p

WAR

- Jenny's War — Jack Stoneley — £1.25
- The Killing-Ground — Elleston Trevor — £1.10

NAVAL HISTORICAL

- The Sea of the Dragon — R. T. Aundrews — 95p
- Ty-Shan Bay — R. T. Aundrews — 95p
- HMS Bounty — John Maxwell — £1.00
- The Baltic Convoy — Showell Styles — 95p
- Mr. Fitton's Commission — Showell Styles — 85p

FILM/TV TIE-IN

- American Gigolo — Timothy Harris — 95p
- Meteor — E. H. North and F. Coen — 95p
- Driver — Clyde B. Phillips — 80p

SCIENCE FICTION

- The Mind Thing — Fredric Brown — 90p
- Strangers — Gardner Dozois — 95p
- Project Barrier — Daniel F. Galouye — 80p
- Beyond the Barrier — Damon Knight — 80p
- Clash by Night — Henry Kuttner — 95p
- Fury — Henry Kuttner — 80p
- Mutant — Henry Kuttner — 90p
- Drinking Sapphire Wine — Tanith Lee — £1.25
- Journey — Marta Randall — £1.00
- The Lion Game — James H. Schmitz — 70p
- The Seed of Earth — Robert Silverberg — 80p
- The Silent Invaders — Robert Silverberg — 80p
- City of the Sun — Brian M. Stableford — 85p
- Critical Threshold — Brian M. Stableford — 75p
- The Florians — Brian M. Stableford — 80p
- Wildeblood's Empire — Brian M. Stableford — 80p
- A Touch of Strange — Theodore Sturgeon — 85p

FICTION

HISTORICAL ROMANCE/ROMANCE/SAGA

☐ Flowers of Fire	Stephanie Blake	£1.00
☐ So Wicked My Desire	Stephanie Blake	£1.50
☐ Morgana	Marie Buchanan	£1.35
☐ The Enchanted Land	Jude Deveraux	£1.50
☐ Mystic Rose	Patricia Gallagher	£1.25
☐ Alinor	Roberta Gellis	£1.20
☐ Gilliane	Roberta Gellis	£1.00
☐ Joanna	Roberta Gellis	£1.25
☐ Roselynde	Roberta Gellis	£1.20
☐ Love's Scarlet Banner	Fiona Harrowe	£1.00
☐ Lily of the Sun	Sandra Heath	95p
☐ Daneclere	Pamela Hill	£1.25
☐ Strangers' Forest	Pamela Hill	£1.00
☐ Royal Mistress	Patricia Campbell Horton	£1.50
☐ The Tall One	Barbara Jefferis	£1.00
☐ Captive Bride	Johanna Lindsey	£1.00
☐ The Flight of the Dove	Catherine MacArthur	95p
☐ The Far Side of Destiny	Dore Mullen	£1.50
☐ The Southern Moon	Jane Parkhurst	£1.25
☐ Summerblood	Anne Rudeen	£1.25
☐ The Year Growing Ancient	Irene Hunter Steiner	£1.10

HORROR/OCCULT/NASTY

☐ The Howling	Gary Brandner	85p
☐ Return of the Howling	Gary Brandner	95p
☐ Dying Light	Evan Chandler	85p
☐ Curse	Daniel Farson	95p
☐ Trance	Joy Fielding	90p
☐ The Janissary	Alan Lloyd Gelb	95p
☐ Rattlers	Joseph L. Gilmore	85p
☐ Slither	John Halkin	95p
☐ Devil's Coach-Horse	Richard Lewis	85p
☐ Spiders	Richard Lewis	80p
☐ Poe Must Die	Marc Olden	£1.00
☐ The Spirit	Thomas Page	£1.00
☐ The Force	Alan Radnor	90p
☐ Bloodthirst	Mark Ronson	90p
☐ Ghoul	Mark Ronson	95p
☐ Ogre	Mark Ronson	95p
☐ Return of the Living Dead	John Russo	80p
☐ The Scourge	Nick Sharman	£1.00
☐ Deathbell	Guy N. Smith	95p
☐ The Specialist	Jasper Smith	85p

WESTERN BLADE SERIES

☐ No. 1	The Indian Incident	Matt Chisholm	75p
☐ No. 2	The Tucson Conspiracy	Matt Chisholm	75p
☐ No. 3	The Laredo Assignment	Matt Chisholm	75p

NAME ....

ADDRESS ....

....

Write to Hamlyn Paperbacks Cash Sales, PO Box 11, Falmouth, Cornwall TR10 9EN.

Please indicate order and enclose remittance to the value of the cover price plus:

U.K.: 30p for the first book, 15p for the second book and 12p for each additional book ordered to a maximum charge of £1.29.

B.F.P.O. & EIRE: 30p for the first book, 15p for the second book plus 12p per copy for the next 7 books, thereafter 6p per book.

OVERSEAS: 50p for the first book plus 15p per copy for each additional book.

Whilst every effort is made to keep prices low it is sometimes necessary to increase cover prices and also postage and packing rates at short notice. Hamlyn Paperbacks reserve the right to show new retail prices on covers which may differ from those previously advertised in the text or elsewhere.